W9-CRI-932

Mustachio

Mustachio

K. Michael and Barbara A. Schmidt

Northwest Publishing, Inc,
Salt Lake City, Utah

Mustachio

All rights reserved
Copyright © 1995 K. Michael and Barbara A. Schmidt

Reproduction in any manner, in whole or in part,
in English or in other languages, or otherwise
without written permission of the publisher is prohibited.

This is a work of fiction.
All characters and events portrayed in this book are fictional,
and any resemblance to real people is purely coincidental.

For information address: Northwest Publishing, Inc.,
6906 South 300 West, Salt Lake City, Utah 84047
BCC 12.31.94

PRINTING HISTORY
First Printing 1995

ISBN 1-56901-448-5

NPI books are published by Northwest Publishing, Inc,
6906 South 300 West, Salt Lake City, Utah 84047
The name "NPI" and the "NPI" logo are trademarks belonging to
Northwest Publishing, Incorporated

PRINTED IN THE UNITED STATES OF AMERICA
10 9 8 7 6 5 4 3 2 1

To Poppy and his loving encouragement.
Here it is at long last.

Contents

Prologue

I'm Dr. Sidney Parker and I learned early on that unusual things always seemed to happen to Joe Calero. Joe Calero, "Mustachio" to a select few, was one of the most remarkable men I have ever met. Complex in the extreme, a study in opposites that pushed and pulled at him from within, promising beauty, danger, love and despair. A man who would draw both gasps and cheers. I was drawn to him, as were so many others who shared the arena of his life.

The first time I saw him was on a hot July day when I paid a visit to old Judge Cash's mansion.

The crunch of gravel under my boots made a comfortable sound as I pushed open a heavy white gate and began the one-mile walk up to the house. It was near four in the afternoon as I started along the dusty lane. The house, an old white mansion, was barely visible since the lane hooked like a bull's horn and disappeared into a stand of mature oak trees just before the house.

A white fence followed the road, stretched out like a mile-long shoot ahead of me, and it held back a grazing bull and some lazing horses. The fence set limits to where I could go unless I wished to risk a brush with the horns. Eyeing the bull, I imagined I could hear the music of the *corrida*. From then on, I would hear it whenever I visited this special place.

It was ten years ago when I made that first walk. The fences needed mending, and other than the bull and the few horses, there seemed to be no other life on what had been Judge Cash's ranch. The place was abandoned then, or so I thought.

The house itself was a turn-of-the-century mansion, built quite far outside of town. It was said that in the old days you could hear music drifting off across the lake and see lights twinkling late into the night. You could hear laughter and, occasionally, the high-pitched voice of a woman lost in delight. It was in coming to the mansion to do a story on old Judge Cash that I was to meet the extraordinary Calero, sometimes called Mustachio—but only by very special people. Suddenly, a man appeared on the porch of the mansion, looming large and looking down at me.

"Hi," I said. "I'm Sidney Parker. I'm doing a story on Judge Cash. You must be...?"

"Calero, the name is Joe Calero. *Buenas tardes, senor.*"

That was the beginning.

1

The Last Mustachio

The old ranch slumbered in the warm California evening. Occasionally, horses stamped their hooves and a distant coyote howled. Nothing disturbed the night except the faint creak of a gate and the crunch of gravel beneath some intruder's feet. The large, shaggy, black dog on the front porch stirred and pricked up his ears. Hearing nothing from his sleeping master, the man Calero, the dog, Spooky, settled back down.

Suddenly there was another sound and Spooky was up and dashing headlong across the lawn, barking loudly. Calero rolled over onto his back, surfacing from a deep sleep, and listened intently to the dog's bark. No, that's not his people-bark, he thought. It may be that damn black stallion down to sniff the mares. God, how Spooky hates that horse. He still has no fear of it even after that kick in the head as a pup. Everyone thought he would be spooky around horses after that, and so he got his name. Just didn't work out that way. Calero chuckled and settled back on the bed, slowly drifting below the surface of consciousness.

There, he was swept into an arena packed with wildly cheering people. Dressed in his "suit of lights" he moved slowly to the center of the bullring as a broad wooden door, heavy with dirt and age, slowly opened and a gigantic force came hurtling from the shoot directly at him.

The bull passed very close. Calero spun on his firmly set black-slippered feet, his heart pounding as the cape drew the animal past and around him. Remaining erect and proud, his head up, he taunted the bull, and the bull charged again. As it brushed against him, Calero could smell the warm wet blood smeared on its hide. He heard the music from the band; he heard the cheering. He moved so close to the bull that now he inhaled its methane breath. He could smell his own fear in the sweat trickling from his armpits. Then the bull charged—and Calero was suddenly awake.

Spooky was barking again, but this time it had a different sound. "Shit. It's his people-bark!" His dream faded away, and Calero wondered whether assholes were dumping garbage on his property again. He rolled onto his back and felt sweat run off his forehead, into his ears and down his neck. He was wide awake and instinctively throwing his right arm across his body, it came to rest against his left side. Then he reached up and pulled a Colt pistol from under his pillow and rested it on his chest.

What am I doing here? Me, descendant of famous bull-fighters! What am I doing in a place like this, hunting garbage-dumpers and lifting fatass *gringos* onto their horses? Damn it! Shut up, Spooky. Who cares? He shouted toward the open window, "I'm coming for you, *pendejos.*"

As he swung his legs over the edge of the bed, the clock slowly chimed 4 A.M. His large barrel-chest heaved with a sigh of resignation as all six-foot-six, two hundred forty pounds of him stood up. Pistol by his side, and with a heavy determined step, he walked to the chair where he'd left his Levi's and boots. Dressing quickly, he finished by buckling on his grandfather's quick-draw holster and the Colt. The old man's words came back to him. "Always on the left, my son, butt end toward the enemy, for a fast draw across your body. Scares them—they back away—they know you know how to use it and that you will."

Spinning the old Colt's chamber, he brought the gun across his body and shoved it snugly into place. Wide awake now, he clumped down the stairs, out the door, and into his white pickup. Spooky was already sitting in the truck bed, quiet and expectant.

Calero slid open the rear window and Spooky jumped into the cab, licked Calero once on the hand and then lay close against his body. Before starting the engine, Calero listened for a moment and determined the sounds the intruders were making came from a different place—different from the usual spot where people illegally dumped their garbage.

"What is it, Spooky? Perhaps poachers this time? We must be careful, my friend; they have guns, you know. But then again, we have Mr. Winchester." He patted the rifle scabbarded against the truck door.

Silence. He listened again for any sounds. Then he heard a distant tap, tap, tap and a slight whine like a very small jet-ski.

He was puzzled. It wasn't a jet-ski but it was a strange sound. "Spooky, what the hell is going on?" The dog sat up, cocked his head, then growled.

It was then Calero spotted headlights at the end of the lane, flicking on and off, on and off. He started the truck and, with no lights on, drove as fast as he dared. When he was close to the gate that closed off the lane, he turned on the pickup's spotlight and directed it at the gate. A man standing there was caught in its glare.

Skidding the pickup to a stop, Calero took in the details. Spooky jumped out the cab window back into the truckbed and began a furious barking.

Holding a fishing pole in his hand and shouting over the dog's barking, the man yelled, "Hey, turn off the damn light—and shut that fucking dog up."

"Why are you trying to crawl over my fence?" Calero demanded.

"I'm just going fishing, mister."

"You're not going fishing on this property, buddy."

"The hell I'm not," said the would-be fisherman, and he started over the fence.

"Just a minute," Calero called out. "Before you crawl over that fence, you got a quarter?"

Stopped by Calero's question, the man paused. "Why?"

"Because if you go over that fence, I'm going to need the quarter to call an ambulance for you."

The man stopped his climb but yelled back, "Oh, big man!"

"You're right. So, get off the fence, get in your car, and get out of here before I sic my dog on you."

Mumbling, the intruder angrily retreated to his car, spun the tires and, in an action that puzzled Calero, flashed his headlights twice. Then he was gone.

"Something isn't right, Spooky." Calero frowned as he stared into the darkness. Then, "Got it! He had no tackle box. No one fishes without a tackle box." Turning the truck around, he drove slowly back, musing, "Where do they come from, these strange intruders in my life? Why me, in this place and time, trapped in this bulky body? Why me, Spooky?"

All was quiet when they returned to the ranch. Calero patted Spooky, and the dog settled down on the office floor. Tossing off a shot of tequila in the old kitchen, Calero clumped back up the stairs, pulled off his boots and fell on the bed. As he tried to drift back into sleep, he thought about his grandfather, *Grande Padre Mustachio*.

"Ah, how I loved that man. What a great bullfighter he was. All of Spain knew his name. Rich and famous, he retired when he was thirty…and then lived to be seventy-five. He was the only man who could do the Pacheco Pass over and over again and live. In my dreams I've tried to do that Pacheco Pass and yet I can't seem to do it. I always wake up. Why can't I do the Pass? Is it because large men never fight bulls? Or because my father tried to do it when he shouldn't have, and he died? Am I afraid to die? Am I afraid to try it even in my dreams?"

Drifting at last into sleep, he dreamt again that he heard the music of the *corrida* proclaiming the beginning of a bull-fight. But exhaustion finally took him beyond the dream to quiet oblivion.

2

Another Typical Day

Calero was awakened when something heavy bounded onto his chest. Then there was a wet tongue on his face. Spooky. Olga must have let him in when she came to work. Olga, the efficient one, always early for work. The one who insisted on getting Calero up and going, even if he'd had a late night. Olga, a tough German woman from Argentina.

Calero tousled his dog's head and gave him a hug. "Good morning, my remarkable animal friend. You spent most of the night chasing horses and people. Brave dog."

Calero thought of the time a stallion had kicked Spooky when he was a pup. "I'm glad that black stallion escaped and now roams free and wild. If he was still around, he'd probably kill one of us. Probably you first, Spooky, with another kick to your head. Then he'd knock my ass into the water trough. He's free like you and I never will be. All the workers think that horse is full of Spanish blood.

"You and me, we've been completely domesticated, my friend. Just like the cattle, just like the riding horses, just like the *gringos*. Everything seems to be recurrent in our lives, like my crazy dream of the bullring, over and over again. I never win, I never lose, and I always sweat. Well, another day at Rancho Calero. Let's go, my friend."

All was quiet downstairs. No Olga, no *nada*. The clock read 6:30 A.M. Calero had forgotten it was he who let the dog in the night before and that when Spooky was ready to get up, everyone had to get up.

Calero warmed old coffee in the microwave, grabbed a stale donut and headed for his truck. The dog raced ahead of him, and Domingo, coming out of the stable, waved and yelled, "Mustachio, take a look at the wheat field down on Old County Road. When you return, we settle the matter about the horse." Calero saluted, a signal that he had heard, and drove off down the lane thinking of Domingo.

Why does he always call me "Mustachio"? I'm not worthy of the name. Grandfather was surely worthy...father, maybe...me? Look at me! A Mustachio? Never!

Shrugging off his morose thoughts as he arrived at the wheat field, Calero felt there was no more beautiful sight, no sweeter smell, than that of a wheat field ready for harvest. Yes, it was ready. Ambling out into the field, Calero left Spooky in the truck, otherwise the dog would take out an acre of harvest chasing ground squirrels.

Scooping up a handful of the wheat heads, Calero smelled them, deeply inhaling the aroma. As he rolled the seeds between his fingers, he could tell this crop would yield one hundredfold. One planted seed would produce another hundred of its kind. It would be the best wheat in the country this year, he was sure of that.

The car phone rang in Calero's white pickup, and Spooky began to bark. "Answer the damn phone, Spooky," Calero yelled as he started back toward the truck. "I wonder if I could teach you to do that?" Then, "Calero here," as he picked up the phone.

"It's Olga. You'd better get back to the ranch. We got a kid crying and a mother on the phone every five minutes wanting us to save a horse that Domingo thinks should have been put down last night."

"I'm on my way." The 454 Chevy engine roared to life. Calero threw the pickup into gear, spinning the tires and throwing dust into the rising sun. The beautiful, bountiful wheat field receded in the rearview mirror.

Calero charged down the lane to the main road and then headed down the highway to the ranch. Winding through the hills, going faster than he should, right on the edge between prudence and recklessness. Reaching the ranch lane, he drove swiftly down the shoot, along the white fences and past the stables, startling some early-morning riders.

At the ranch house, he skidded the truck to a stop, kicked open its door, and burst into the beehive of activity that was the office at Rancho Calero. Speaking to no one, he went directly to a little boy sitting on one of the office chairs, a red-haired nine-year-old whose eyes were swollen with grief, his freckled face set in resignation.

"There's a Nola Rodriguez on the phone," Olga announced. "Sounds like you should know who she is. A 'Miss VIP Panties'…or I miss my guess."

"Tell her I'll call back."

Olga covered the mouthpiece. "This woman acts like she's really somebody—Miss Uppity."

"Later."

Olga persisted. "You've got twenty-five people going out on a ride today and…"

Ignoring her, Calero put his arm around the boy. "Come on, son. Let's you and I take a little walk."

They headed out toward the edge of the lake, and no one could hear what Calero was saying, but Domingo, standing out by the barn, knew what it was. He fetched Calero's rifle and prepared it, then waited and watched as Calero, down on his haunches, shifted a sprig of hay to the corner of his mouth and continued talking to the boy.

When Calero at last returned to the office, the boy was still with him. Olga looked at them questioningly and announced, "That Nola Rodriguez called again."

"Jesus Christ, Olga. Sorry...excuse me, Johnny. Olga, take '42' out of that rental string. He belongs to Johnny now."

"We can't do that, Calero, we're already short on horses for the ride this morning."

"Can't help that. Johnny just bought 42, didn't you, son?"

The boy nodded his head in agreement.

Olga looked disapproving. "And how much should I post to the books?"

Calero smiled. "This is a private matter between Johnny and me, Olga. We'll talk about it later."

Olga rolled expressive eyes. "Oh, Jesus."

Calero turned to Mary, the tall, serious, energetic high-school senior who worked in the office for the summer.

"Mary, take Johnny to get some cookies and milk. If he's going to go out to be with his new friend, we don't want him to go out hungry, do we?" Mary bounded out of the room and headed for the kitchen with the boy in tow.

Phones were ringing, people were coming in, and Olga spoke to a woman who had just walked in and wanted to board two horses. The woman wanted to talk to Calero personally, and turning to her, Calero said, "Just as soon as I take care of an important matter, ma'am, I'll be at your service. You'll have to excuse me for just a few minutes." Tipping his big white felt hat, he walked out the door.

He headed across the yard toward the bunkhouse. Domingo, who had been waiting for him picked, up the rifle, put it in the crook of his arm and fell in with Calero. They walked to the end stall of the stable. A small cluster of riders had gathered there and began giving unsolicited advice.

"I think the horse is going to be all right if we can just get him up, if we can just…" one of them started to say.

"I'd like you all to leave now," Calero commanded quietly.

"You're not going to hurt that horse or anything, are you? You should get a vet out here."

Calero walked over and patted the horse, touching and studying its injured leg. Then he turned to Domingo. "Agreed, my friend?"

"Agreed, Mustachio."

"Then clear out these people. They don't appear to agree with us."

"*Adios, amigos. Adios, adios. Fuera, fuera,*" urged Domingo, herding people before him like a mother hen clucking her chicks away from danger. By the time he had them all away from the row of stalls, they heard a shot. Everyone froze.

"Jesus, he killed that horse and didn't even call the vet. What the hell kind of person is he?" One of the new boarders was demanding an answer.

"He is a person who loves horses…a person who *knows* horses. One person who doesn't wait to call up his courage while an animal suffers." Domingo turned away. Calero walked past him glumly, handed him the Winchester, and started back to the house.

By the time he had returned to the swirling activity of the office, he was ready to take on the next task.

"You gave the horse to that boy, didn't you?" Olga stated as he walked in. "To make up for having to shoot his injured one."

"I'd give anybody a horse, long as they promised to buy their hay from me. Johnny promised."

Olga shook her head. "How many times have I heard that?"

Calero smiled briefly, and turning to the woman he had asked to wait, he listened to her request. "About boarding my horses, Mr. Calero. Could I get a break if I bring two horses here instead of one? Also, I have plenty of money, but I'd like to wait until the end of the month to pay you."

Calero looked closely at her, uneasy about her request. "Tell me, ma'am, where are your horses now?"

"Well, they're over at my house, in the hauling trailer. My boyfriend's going to bring them over just as soon as I call him."

"Where did you have the horses before?" Calero asked.

She acted offended. "I don't know why that's any of your business."

"Ma'am, did Jack Nord ask you to leave his stable?"

"What business is that of yours?"

"You're asking me for credit. All I'm doing is a little credit check. I'd like to know where you've had the horses before. I'd like to call there and then we'll talk to Olga here about making you a loan."

"Well, I've never heard such crap. You'll hear from me again." Furious, the woman left, slamming the screen door behind her.

"Hey, Calero, now that was good business." Olga was pleased, but added, "You know you're going to hear from the jerk who runs the park commission."

"I know, but I'm not going to get stuck with a couple of eatin' machines that are owned by a woman I'm sure doesn't pay her bills. And I'm sure she has a super-flake trouble-maker for a boyfriend."

"You have no way of knowing that, Calero."

"Trust me, Olga, I know."

"Okay, okay, but why 42 to that boy? He's our best trail horse."

"Well, Johnny's our best boarder."

"Come on, Calero. He's only one of seventy kids here. You don't even know him."

"I know every one of the kids and I know Johnny's a good kid, maybe the best of the lot. He's agreed to work for me and I know he'll do a good job. 42 deserves a boy like Johnny. Olga, that kid knew what had to be done to his horse before anybody else did, and he asked me to do it for him. That's a boy with a solid future. He knows what needs to be done, but he also knows his limitations. I can't help but love a boy like that, Olga."

3

Incident at Calero Lake

In an attempt to escape the confusion in the office, Calero decided he could use a short ride. Saddling his horse, he rode off toward the lake. Then he saw the buckskin's ears shoot forward and felt the quiver that ran over its body. Calero pulled back gently on the reins as the peace of the misty morning was shattered by the screams of two young girls. Probably the same two he had seen set out for a ride some-time earlier.

There was another scream, too—a mechanical one. The prick of Mexican spurs sent the horse plunging down the hill toward the lake, the screams, and two onrushing horses.

Heading off the frightened runaways was child's play for Calero, but he was angered at the cause of their fright. Calming the girls, he told them to lead their horses the short distance back to the ranch and once there to tell Domingo what had happened.

As they started off, the mechanical scream continued and Calero galloped around the lake in the direction of the sound. Pulling the buckskin to a stop, Calero yelled at the young blond boy plowing across the lake astride a jet-ski. "Hey, you, you scared those horses…you're trespassin'…and you've pissed me off!"

Unafraid, the boy sneered at the imposing Spaniard who nearly dwarfed the buckskin he rode. "Eat it, Pancho," he yelled, flipping Calero the bird. Then, in an effort to make a macho escape from the confrontation, the boy throttled the machine too hard, too fast, and it leapt into the air, spilling its rider into the clear, cold water. That was all the time Calero needed. Spurring the horse forward, he threw his swirling rope over the jet-ski and pulled it to shore.

The throttle had jammed on high speed and the screaming engine begged to be silenced. *No problema.* Calero drew his Winchester from its case on the left side of the saddle. One shot rang out, and the earlier peace of the morning was restored.

Back at the ranch, the two girls were startled by the shot, but a reassuring and knowing smile brushed across the weathered face of old Domingo. "Do not worry, little ones, there is no problem."

Later, when Calero returned, he had instructions for Domingo. "Send Otillio and another man down to the lake with the pickup. There's a carcass there for them to dispose of. Oh, yeah...and have them bring the blond kid with the chipped tooth back here. I think he needs a ride back to where he came from."

Calero left Domingo and headed to the ranch office, arriving in time to hear Olga groan, "Oh, geez, another damn phone call." She picked up the receiver, listened for a moment, then turned to Calero. "Some guy who has two horses to board would like to bring them right over. What should I tell him?"

"Tell him we're full up. It's got to be that woman's flakey boyfriend—the woman who tried to dump her two nags on me for free."

"But we've got four empty stalls."

"Not any more."

Olga returned to the caller. "Sorry, sir, we don't have any stalls available at this time. If you'd like to leave your name I can give you a call when we have an opening." She paused and her eyes widened. "There's no need to talk to me like that, sir. Well, you just do that." The receiver went down hard.

"Guess you were right, Calero. Hey, can you sign these checks? I have to get to the bank. And where the hell is Mary? Still in the kitchen with Johnny or what?" Olga gave out a yell, "Mary, get in here and take these phones. Oh, God, there they go again."

This time her eyebrows raised as she answered one of the ringing phones. "Oh, yes, Miss Rodriguez, he just walked in. He can't wait to take your call. One moment, please." Pressing the hold button, Olga held out the receiver and Calero took it, ignoring Olga's smirk.

"Calero, here. Well, how do you do, Nola Rodriguez. How can I help you? I see. You have a palomino stallion and a pet heifer you'd like to board at my stables. Unfortunately, ma'am, we have about one hundred eighty pleasure horses and another twenty-five...make that twenty-four...in the rental string, and I don't know how many of them are mares. I know if they see that beautiful palomino of yours, with his equipment intact, they'll all go nuts.

"I know, I know, Miss Rodriguez, I'd certainly like to help you, but I also have seventy children here for summer camp and...well, I'm sorry you feel that way. The Triangle Sand and Gravel Company? Well, I certainly have heard of it. That's one proud company you have there. I've heard very good things about it and I see your trucks everywhere. I sure would like to make an exception for you but I just can't." Calero listened as his caller continued her efforts to persuade him. "Why, yes, I could meet with you. Perhaps coffee in town...? Or why don't you come out here and I'll show you around the stables. I'm sure you'll understand then why your

Mustachio

stallion…yes, I'm willing to discuss it further but you understand…I see, ma'am. Well, you have a nice day now."

He hung up the phone and Olga said, "Oh, gag me. I just saw the great Spaniard sink low enough to kiss that Rodriguez woman's butt."

"Olga, be nice, be nice."

Finally returning to the office, Mary announced she was going to take Johnny to get 42 out of the string, but Olga snapped at her, "Oh, no you're not. Johnny knows perfectly well where the horse is and how to handle him. You take these damn telephones, Mary!"

"But, Johnny…"

"Forget it, Mary. You just sit here with these phones. I've got to go to the bank. Calero, get over here and sign these checks, for godsakes. Oh, yes, I nearly forgot." Glancing over at two Mexicans sitting quietly in one corner of the office, she told them in perfect Spanish, "You can go to work. See Domingo and tell him to put you back to work."

"Gracias, senora, gracias."

"And remember, no pay until Friday—a week from this Friday, and you work today free. *Comprende?"*

"Si, senora."

"What the hell was that all about?" Calero wanted to know as the men left the office.

"I haven't time to explain now. Sign these checks and I'm gone. The county has to have its pound of flesh today, you know." Olga shook her head in disgust. "Jesus, I hate paying those bastards twenty percent of our gross. Who the hell ever made that contract with them? Oh. Sorry, *Don* Calero. And one more thing. Two notes in the suggestion box. Both say you should be feeding the horses more alfalfa and less oat hay. Not signed. Neither of them."

"Must be the twins again." Calero smiled.

Olga nodded her head in agreement. "I figured it was them."

"Those two talk to their horses and insist the horses understand them," Calero snorted. "Don't they know a horse's brain is about as big as its ear? I'll just tell Domingo to pop in an extra flake of alfalfa each day. Those horses are already too fat. I've never seen it to fail—fat master, fat horse. Now, anything else?"

"Well, you know those six heifers you bought against my advice? You better get some of that 'pregnancy interruptus' material from the vet. What's-his-name…the one who sold you the heifers…called and said he thinks maybe his prize bull nailed some of them before you bought them."

"Oh, God," Calero moaned, hitting his forehead and knocking his hat back on his head. "How far along did he say they might be?"

"Probably not more than a month or so," Olga answered, concern in her voice.

Rubbing the back of his neck and pushing his hat back on top of his head Calero thought a moment, then said, "If we abort them, they may have problems; and if we don't, for sure they will have big problems. Well, if one of them kicks the bucket, its carcass is going to end up on that guy's doorstep…I can promise you that!" He faced the waiting Olga. "Call the vet and tell him I want to pick up enough Lutalyse this afternoon for six heifers. This can't wait."

"So much for your 'cattle are money in the bank,' Calero. That Lutalyse will set you back plenty…and one of the heifers will probably give birth anyway and then die because the calf was too big for her."

"Thanks a lot, Olga. Any more problems? I can hardly wait."

Olga shuffled through some phone messages on her desk. "The Chinaman said to meet him at Sinnobar Hills Coffee

Shop at noon tomorrow. He'll buy lunch…and give you the back rent he owes you for that piece of land you leased him. Oh, yes, then there's that public hearing on Rancho Calero. You might want to go and see what's going on."

"Did the county send back that lease on the stable yet?"

"Nope, and I bet they don't," she snorted as she headed for the door. "Back in two hours. Mary, don't you leave this office under any circumstances. You have to go to the bathroom first?"

"No, ma'am."

"Well, you have your orders, sweetheart."

"I know," Mary said, and watched as Olga patted at her hair as if reminding her "do" of its proper place. "And don't forget to meet that man Newell behind the coffee shop at eleven."

"Got it on my list, Mary."

"Who's Newell?" Calero asked.

"Never mind. You don't want to know," Olga tossed over her shoulder, and banged out the door.

"Whoa, she's a tough one. And, gee, Mr. Calero, can she ever speak Spanish. I didn't know that. Those two Mexican fellows who were in here were saying something, and I'll tell you she sure got hot and she chewed them out in Spanish. They darn near fell through the floor. Boy, I wish I understood Spanish. I'd love to know what that was all about."

Calero smiled, thinking about Olga. "Mary, I'm going down to check on the rental string. We're going to have a couple of cranky riders when they find out we're two horses short…and I want to make sure Johnny gets 42 cut out of there…and gets a stall on another part of the ranch. I don't want him to have to go near the old one." Calero thought a moment and fired off another order. "Oh, and call the renderer to come pick up the horse I had to shoot."

"Call the who?"

"Look under 'Rendering' on the Rolodex."

Mary flipped through the cards until she found it. "Here it is...Oh!"

"Yeah, that poor horse is going to the glue factory and I don't want Johnny to see it."

"Okay, Mr. Calero, I'll call right away."

As Calero started out the door, one of the boarders—an attractive, shapely woman—managed to accidentally-on-purpose bump into him. "Well, hello! And how are you this lovely day?" Her tone was inviting as she looked him up and down.

"Just fine, ma'am, I'm just fine." And he tipped his hat in her direction.

"I'll bet you are." She smiled, admiring his patrician features as he passed her. She let out her breath slowly and rolled her eyes as she entered the office. "What a hunk!" she murmured.

Chuckling to himself, Calero moved off the porch, and the woman who had brushed past him turned her attention to Mary. "For starters, Mary, could you tell me, woman to woman, how I could get to first base with your big hunk boss? He's as handsome as he is big, and I just love his mustache. Very sexy."

"Well, I wouldn't know about that woman to woman stuff, ma'am. Mr. Calero is very nice and proper, and he doesn't date the boarders. He is a big man, all right...and I believe his father was a real bullfighter...or something like that. Nobody pushes Mr. Calero around...except maybe Olga."

"Oh, are they an item?" The woman looked disappointed.

"Good heavens, no!" Mary laughed, putting her hand over her face. "It's just that Olga thinks he's too nice to people...gives them things they don't deserve. He is mighty generous, I'll say that for him. And all the guys that work here respect him and like him a lot—especially old Domingo. Olga says that old man would die for Mr. Calero."

The woman smiled at Mary. "Actually, I just wanted to drop off my boarding check. But tell me, does he always wear expensive western boots?"

"Yep, and that bugs Olga, too. Tony Lama boots, fancy jeans, and tailored jackets. 'A Spaniard with the tastes of a rich bullfighter and the brains of a bull.' That's what Olga says about him. To his face, too! Yep. She says he's the last of a dying breed...whatever that means."

"It means I'd better hurry and get my hands on him if he's the last of his kind." The boarder gave Mary a sly smile, then headed out the door.

4

A Chance Meeting

The hearing had gone badly. The coffee tasted bitter to Calero and burned the lining of his stomach, and the old cafe, recently remodeled, was crowded and not to his liking. I need tequila in my veins and the taste of lime in my mouth, not this black swill. Kiss your riding stable and your dream good-bye, Calero.

That's what the hearing had added up to. Slick lawyers and the twerp mayor had played the parks department off against the county water department and hadn't given the riding public even the time of day. The Riders' Association had received only five minutes!

"Five minutes!" Calero said it out loud as he banged his fist on the counter. His coffee cup jumped and the spoon in his saucer sang out in protest.

Looking up, he found others in the shop staring at him. He didn't much care. Sitting taller and raising his strong chin just a little, he smiled and apologized to the Mexican lad sitting two stools down from him. That was when the woman by the window caught his eye. She was staring, her dark, penetrating eyes fixed on him.

Leaning forward just a little, his vision flooded with her beautiful face, he smiled and tilted his head. She made no response but continued to stare, her red lips slightly parted. For a moment, unsure, he looked away.

Must be losing my grip, he thought. I didn't even see her when I walked by the window.

She, on the other hand, had watched him closely as, strutting across the street from the courthouse, he had entered the coffee shop and, with a dismissive air, took a stool at the counter. Just arrogant enough to be attractive, she thought. She was struck by his full head of shining black hair, combed straight back and neatly trimmed as though he had just slipped out of the barber's chair.

She wasn't sure about the mustache. It was neat, but made him seem distant and perhaps not to be trusted. Tight-fitting tailored clothes, black gloves tucked into his belt, and highly polished boots completed the picture. She liked this piece of work. It was going to be interesting meeting this Spaniard who still sat straight and proud despite the beating he'd taken in that arena across the street.

She had studied him long and close at the courthouse hearing. Sitting off to one side she could tell that this man, Calero, was absorbed and oblivious to those who gaped at him. His whole being reflected intense concentration.

There's a man who doesn't miss a thing—a dangerous man, perhaps. I shall will him now…will him to come to me. There, the eyes have it. Locked! Hold it. Now, smile! Gotcha!

Calero nodded and touched two fingers to the side of his face in salute. That dark beauty is putting the moves on me. So goes the great matador to his prey! *Ole!*

Swinging smoothly on his stool to face the woman by the window, all six-foot-six of Calero rose and moved across the room.

"Buenos dias, senorita. Joe Calero, *a sus ordenes."*

"Really? You're at my service?" Nola played coy. At Calero's gallant nod, she continued, "We shall see, Mr. Calero. First, please sit down. Maybe after I know you better, I'll let you help me with some of my little problems." A smile flickered across her mouth and her eyes danced. She leaned forward just enough so that the swell of her breasts made it difficult for Calero to stay focused on her face.

"I'm Nola. Nice to meet you. When I saw you come in, I realized from your clothes that you probably know cattle and horses, so perhaps you could help me with one of my problems. I have this sick cow, and the vet has been out several times but tells me there's nothing wrong with the animal. I don't believe him...the cow doesn't have a happy face any more, and she's awfully thin."

"How old is this cow?" Calero asked her.

"Well, she's just a heifer. She's a pet and I call her Baby Face. I've been awfully busy lately and haven't spent much time with her. Maybe she's lonely? She doesn't seem to be eating."

"I take it Baby Face is living alone?" Calero asked.

"Well," Nola said, "my horse is out in the pasture with her, but he's a bit rambunctious and always on the run. She can't keep up with him."

"I see. What you have, Nola, is an animal with a strong herding instinct and no herd. She'll never do well until she's part of one." He wanted to impress her and felt pleased with himself so far. His chin did a typical upward tilt. "What have you been feeding her?"

"Just the grass she's grazing on...and some oat hay."

"Hm-m. Loneliness can take the edge off an animal's appetite...it can also take the edge off people's," Calero offered philosophically. "Would you agree?"

"Oh, yes." Nola replied, leaning forward eagerly. "Loneliness can be a strange thing. I think it's possible to even be in love, and yet still be lonely."

"Well, Nola, I don't even know your last name, but are you in love...and lonely?"

"My God, you're forthright!" Nola sat back in her chair. "No. I'm not in love, but at times I am lonely. Are you?"

Calero paused. "Yes, in a way. I guess all of us are lonely until we find our soulmate...or someone of the opposite sex who's like us. I read somewhere that it's our opposite side we are looking for...and we'll never be complete or whole until we find it."

"Oh," said Nola, "I know. I just think most men simply marry mother figures...and women, a father one."

"That probably happens. Maybe we just don't take the time to figure out what we really need to bring some kind of balance and harmony into our lives." Calero paused, then asked, "Nola, have you lived in these parts very long?"

"Yes, all my life. It's strange we've never met."

"Perhaps we've been on opposite sides of the arena." He surveyed her clothing, enjoying the chance it gave him to observe her body as well. "Yes, from the way you dress, I would say that you sit on the shaded side of the arena...while I sit in the sun."

"Oh, come on, *Don* Calero, don't give me that 'poor Mexican' routine. You're too arrogant to be poor. You're wearing a five-hundred-dollar pair of boots...and gloves that look like they're handmade. I'll bet when you go to the bullfights, you sit squarely in the shade."

"Well," he said as he smiled, "that's true. In fact, I usually sit in the *oficionado* box or stand down with those who raise the bulls."

"You do? That sounds fascinating."

"Perhaps we can experience a bullfight together one of these days. Have you ever been?"

"No. I hate them because of the cruelty to the bulls."

Calero frowned. "Ah...the response of one who does not understand."

Nola felt a flash of anger. Had he seen it? Arrogant bastard. Be calm, she told herself. You're getting your hooks in nicely.

But Calero had noticed. M-m-m. This one gets angry easily. Don't push her too much...don't want to delay the ultimate thrill.

His tone was placating when he spoke. "Forgive me, my new friend, I didn't mean to offend you. It's just that so few people understand the art and ritual of the bullfight. I've heard what you said...about the cruelty to the bull...so many times. Perhaps I can explain it to you sometime so you will see it differently." Calero felt it wise then to change the subject. "Does your family live here, too?"

Nola sighed. "My father was a businessman. He was like you—big and proud. He's dead now. He was my friend, and I loved him very much. He gave me everything—I guess he spoiled me. Maybe that's why I can't find my soulmate. I just can't seem to find a man like my father—one who gave me everything, but never anything I didn't need."

Nola paused and sighed again. "You know, I always felt I didn't need many things from my father. It was just enough to be around him, to have him hug me...he was always there for me. I thought our lives would go on forever. We had to say good-bye many times, but I never got to say the final good-bye to him. He never told me he was..."

She seemed unable to finish the thought, but after a moment continued, "My mother died early on and it was very hard on my father. I always feared something might happen to him. He was wonderful, so powerful, successful. I guess, in many ways, I thought of him as a god...and, if he was, that no force could ever take him from us."

Calero frowned slightly, then asked, "You said 'us.' Who is 'us'?"

"Oh, I meant my brother, Frank, and me. Frank didn't take our father's death as hard as I did...in fact, he almost seemed relieved. You see, only Frank, the company president, and some of his advisors knew my father was ill. It was a best-kept secret—almost the best."

There was sadness in Nola's frown before she went on. "You would have liked my father and he would have liked you, Calero. You're his kind of man. He dressed well...always immaculate." She took one of Calero's hands. "See how clean your hands are. That's very unusual for a person who works as hard as you do. It's almost as though your nails are manicured. I often wondered how my father managed that look."

Calero was intrigued. "How do you know I work so hard?"

"Oh, I know. I hear things. I have a horse and I'm in the Riders' Association. They talk about the great Calero and Rancho Calero. You know, some say you've wasted your talents there...that you're wasting your efforts on the riding stable...on farming and cattle."

He looked at her quizzically, thinking that this woman seemed to know a whole lot about him.

Nola broke in on his thoughts then to ask about his father, and Calero was quick to respond. "Oh, yes, my father. He died young, much too young. He was a bullfighter."

"You're kidding me! A bullfighter? Why aren't you a bullfighter?" Nola's face was alight with curiosity. "You could be rich and famous."

"Rich and famous, and perhaps dead. But, when you wear size twelve boots, you can't be a bullfighter. They don't make matador slippers that big," he said, and he laughed.

Nola laughed with him. "You've a nice sense of humor, Mr. Calero. I would be willing to learn something about bullfighting if you would teach me, particularly since...since you lost your father that way. I'd like to hear the story sometime. Does it hurt you much to talk about your father?"

"No, Nola, that doesn't hurt. What does hurt is to talk about my grandfather, who was also a bullfighter. He left me not too long ago."

"Was he an old man, Calero?"

"Yes, but not very old. He was seventy-five."

When Nola asked how his grandfather had died, Calero told her it was a story for another time. "It's hard for me to talk about *Grande Padre Mustachio*. Ah, how I still love him."

Calero looked out the window toward the hills, his mind filled with memories. His vision began to blur as he heard the music again. He saw the bull curling around *Grande Padre Mustachio*'s body, the cape swirling in a death-defying Pacheco Pass. Then instantly, the music was silenced by Nola's question. "Were you with him just now?"

"Yes," Calero barely whispered it. "My family has a long history of fighting the bulls in Spain...and a shorter one of fighting them in the Americas. I was told that two hundred years ago my great-great-grandfather was the first man to fight a bull on foot. The men in my family have always taken great risks, and some paid the ultimate price—their lives."

"I see we have a lot in common—Spanish blood, Spanish language...Spanish eyes." Nola looked deep into Calero's eyes.

"The song, 'Spanish Eyes'...do you like it?" he asked her.

When Nola replied that it was one of her favorites, Calero walked across the room toward the jukebox intending to play the record. It was then he realized the coffee shop was deserted. Glancing at the wall clock, he saw the time. They had been talking for nearly two hours.

Finding the song on the jukebox, Calero pushed the button for two plays. The music of "Spanish Eyes" began to fill the air. Nola leaned back in her chair, long legs stretched out, arms behind her head, her slender, curvaceous body at ease.

When Calero returned to the table she asked him if he liked to dance. "Or are you like most of the cowboys—'Cotton-Eye Joe'...and that sort of thing?"

"I can dance a little," Calero admitted.

"I love to rhumba. My father sent me for dancing lessons…my brother Frank, too. We're both very good dancers. Can you rhumba?"

Calero was confident. "I'm sure I can with you, Nola." He made a mental note to find a dance studio the very next day.

5

Nola's Arena

Calero knew he wanted to get Nola to himself. The sooner he got her out of the coffee shop the better. He decided to use the heifer, Baby Face, as his excuse. "Where would a girl like you keep a pet heifer?" he asked.

"Just ten miles outside town. Actually, it's on the way out to your ranch," she admitted casually.

"Hey, that's good. Let's drive out that way and I'll see what I can do for Baby Face. At least, if I come along it will add to her herd." Encouraged by Nola's laughter, he added, "Oh, by the way, I didn't get your last name."

Nola grinned at him. "I didn't give it."

"Oh, mysterious," he said, and his brow wrinkled.

"Yes, I think mystery makes life more exciting, Mr. Calero, don't you? I think there are some mysteries about you, too."

Calero could feel anticipation rising in him. Her remarks had him intrigued. He stood and extended his hand to help her from her chair, and when she accepted it, it was all he could do to keep from pulling her to him.

After he paid the bills, he moved smoothly to one side and a bit ahead of Nola. *"Permitame,"* he murmured, and bowing slightly, he ushered her out the door.

As she passed by him, he took in her black gaucho-style hat—nice touch. The red scooped-neck blouse revealing the peekaboo black lace of her bra was another nice touch. And her long lovely legs ended in expensive, red, tooled boots.

What a woman, what a figure! If that body is crying out for help, I would like it to know that help is on the way!

Following Nola toward a yellow Cadillac Alante, parked by an expired meter, Calero helped her in on the driver's side. Then he walked to his truck and removed a ticket from under one of his wiper blades as the Alante roared by. My God, but she drove fast!

Ten miles out of town and following Nola, Calero saw the directional signal flash on her Alante and the brake lights illuminated as her car turned left. Nola drove through a wide steel gate opened by remote control, and Calero followed her down a dusty lane. As his truck cleared the gate, it began to close automatically. I like that, he thought.

Then, out of the corner of his eye, he saw the sign on the gate: Triangle Sand and Gravel Company. Oh, oh, I've got it now. This is none other than Nola "telephone-Olga-gag me" Rodriguez. M-m-m-m. Yep, there's her Palomino tearing up and down the field, balls blowing in the wind…all excited about seeing his mistress. There's a tornado of a horse just waiting to cause a human disaster. This woman must love to play dangerous games. But this certainly can't be where she lives…that old farmhouse and the barn are in good condition, but no Triangle Sand and Gravel lady would live here.

Calero pulled up beside the Alante now parked by the barn. Nola had already gone over to the fence to pet the Palomino, and she was obviously giving him some sugar. She talks to that horse as if talking to a person. Strange how some women are about their damn horses.

Over by the barn he spotted what he assumed was Baby Face. Walking over to a nearby fence, he rested his foot on a rail and studied the heifer as it walked toward him. Malnutrition, or I miss my guess. Putting on his gloves, he opened the gate and went over to the heifer. "Now, my friendly little gal, how are you?"

As he examined Baby Face, Nola arrived, bringing a flake of oat hay which she threw down. The heifer ignored it. Calero, however, chose to examine the hay, running it between his fingers to judge its quality. "This is good quality oat hay, Nola, but this heifer needs alfalfa. I'll see you get some."

The Palomino trotted over just then, sniffed at the heifer, spun around and ran off, kicking his heels in the air as he went. "Some stallion you got there, Miss Rodriguez. Now, why didn't you tell me who you were?"

Nola smiled at him. "Because I wanted you to get to know me for myself, not for my name. Maybe I just wanted you to like me for being me."

"Well, you've succeeded, Nola Rodriguez. How about I make a deal with you? I'll take the heifer. After she's fattened up a little, I'll put her in with my herd...but you keep the Palomino."

Anger flashed across Nola's face and she stamped her red-booted foot. "That won't do! That's not what I want. I want you to take the Palomino, too."

"I'm just trying to help you, Nola," Calero said, and he turned away, as Nola, obviously piqued, walked determinedly over to the barbed-wire fence. She jerked her hand back suddenly from the fence and Calero knew immediately what had happened. Without a word, he went to his truck. Returning, he removed his gloves, reached out his right hand and commanded, "Give me your hand, Nola."

He knew she had cut it on the barbed wire. "Had your tetanus shot?" When she snapped back that she had, he gently commanded again, "Let me see that hand."

As she laid her hand in his, Nola became very aware of the smooth texture of his cheeks and forehead, and especially his lips.

Tenderly, Calero dabbed at her cut hand with disinfectant, stopped the bleeding, and covered the cut with a Band-Aid. It really wasn't much of a cut, but Nola stood in front of him looking like a helpless child. She'd become angry and she got hurt.

Touched, he stretched out his arms. "Nola, let me hug you. My grandmother used to say that a hug helps the healing." She was soft but stiff when he pulled her to him. Calero could feel her breasts beneath the red blouse. He longed to have her thighs and stomach pressed against him but they remained withdrawn. Pulling away from him, Nola walked toward her car, then stopped. Turning, she met his eyes. "I don't want you to think I didn't like being hugged, Calero. I did like it…but you caught me by surprise."

She walked back to him then and put her arms around him. This time he felt her whole body against him. The smell of her sweetly perfumed hair, mixed with the fragrance of her skin, created a deep arousal in Calero. His heart quickened.

That was when Nola pushed him away playfully and said, "Come on, it's getting late. I have to go home." She ran over to her car and slid into the driver's seat. As Calero closed the door after her, he said, "I'll see you."

Nola nodded quietly. "I know."

"I'll take another look at the heifer before I leave…and I'll have some alfalfa sent over. I'll close up for you, too. Just tell me how to operate that front gate."

Once Nola had explained how the gate worked, Calero waved her off, then turned back toward the barn and the heifer. Patting Baby Face, he said, "You know, we need to get you fattened up and out of here. I'll be back."

Once back in his truck, he phoned Rancho Calero. Olga answered and inquired about the hearing, which he promised to tell her about later. "Right now, Olga, have Domingo send ten bales of TDN alfalfa over to 2626 Old Monterey Road.

Tell him he can open the gate by pressing a switch on the left side of the gate, third rail down...no, it's the bottom third rail...underneath is a little switch. All he has to do is press it and the gate will open."

"Who should I bill for the hay, Calero? And, did you say TDN—that expensive, high-protein, total-digestible nutrients stuff?"

Olga's questions showed she knew more than routine office procedures, and Calero smiled to himself. "Yes, that stuff, and bill it to my account. I need to pay a debt." Olga wanted the name of the customer, but Calero told her, "You don't want to know, Olga!" And then he hung up.

Driving home, Calero was thinking that the feel of Nola's body during that second hug was worth the price of ten bales of hay. I'd give a whole barn full of hay just to do it one more time. Nola Rodriguez...what a beauty. Sure would like to have her riding around my ranch, but then again, maybe we'd better not mix business with pleasure.

Jesus, that stallion of hers. She's going to get herself killed. Well, if she wanted to bring him to my ranch she'd have to cut that horse's balls off. It wouldn't calm him much but it would sure make a big difference to all my mares. Wonder what I ought to tell her? Two times now I've seen her flash with anger. I have a feeling this lady doesn't like any interference with what she wants. Well, now she's met the great bullfighter, Calero, and he is going to cape her right into bed. We'll see how willful she is after that.

6

Just an Old Lady's Funeral

The wheat harvest is going well, Calero thought. Seventy-five bushels to the acre, according to Domingo's estimate. It'll go higher. He wheeled Buck around and galloped back toward the ranch along Dead Cow Trail. He was feeling great now that the harvest had begun and money would start flowing in. He slowed the horse to a walk. There's no hurry, no worry. Take it easy—enjoy the moment.

He rode up on Sinnobar Hill and surveyed the land below him. What a view. The whole valley, the beautiful ranch. I wish it was mine, big Buck, all mine. But, there's a cloud in the sky over Sinnobar Hills and one in my mind…but they are small and nonthreatening on this perfect day.

Calero sat proudly on his horse, looking out over his dude ranch, and wondering again what a Spaniard descended from famous bullfighters was doing in a place like this. Chuckling, he thought of how *Grande Padre Mustachio* had caped many bulls into permanent retirement. Ah, he thought regretfully, to have lived at that time and fought in the great arenas.

But it is only the bulls in my mind I can cape. I hear the music for the beginning of the corrida…but never the triumphant music at the end. Over and over, I cape the bull…but I never make a kill.

Calero nudged his horse, and the two moved as one as they descended the hill toward the old mansion and the daily demands and buzz of activity there. "Well, Buck, life seems okay for now. The harvest is coming in. *Ole!*" he was shouting as he came up to the stables.

"Good harvest, *mi amigo,*" offered Domingo as he took Calero's sweaty horse.

"And good life?"

"*Tal vez. Tal vez,*" Domingo responded as he led Buck away.

Still in high spirits, Calero bounded up the stairs of the house, crossed the porch and entered the office.

"Great harvest, Olga. It'll go eighty to ninety bushels to the acre. The gold will be pouring into the wagons and all is well!" Spinning around in a tight circle, fanning the air, he imitated the famous Pacheco Pass. Strutting around the office, head in the air, an arrogant look splashed across his features, he suddenly stopped. Olga's face and body were sending a message that arrested his mood and made his stomach knot in concern.

"What's up, Olga? Why so glum?" he queried, and watched as she pushed herself slowly away from the desk and rose as though lifting an overweight bale of hay.

"Ah, Joe," she half-whispered, and moved toward him shaking her head slowly.

Now standing straight and stiff, he awaited her. Then her strong hands gripped his shoulders and the big German woman stared into his face. "Miss Julie called and could hardly talk. She kept asking for you. Then she told me…her sister, Sarah, died in her sleep last night. Julie found her this morning. I'm so sorry, Joe. I know the old lady meant a lot to you."

Calero swallowed hard and tried to pull away, but Olga held fast to his huge arms. She looked intently into his darkening Spanish face and sent a message of love and concern to him as she saw his eyes flood with tears. "When's the service?" he managed to choke out.

"Wednesday, Santa Clara Mission…at five in the afternoon, Joe."

"Oh, Olga. So soon, so sudden…so final!"

Olga released her hold on his arms, and he slumped against the door, his face buried in his forearm. They were both silent for a time. No one came in and they were left alone. Mercifully, the phones hung silent in their cradles. The reality of death, the impact of friends and loved ones lost, and these shared moments of silence, brought the two of them even closer together. Two unique people who understood each other. They cared for each other far more than anyone would suspect.

At last Calero moved. "A walk—I need a walk now." He called to his dog, "Spooky, Spooky!" Then not looking at Olga or saying anything to her, he headed off toward the lake as Spooky rushed to his side.

Once he was gone, Olga whispered after him, "I love you, Joe, I love you." Tears filled her steel-blue eyes, now soft with concern.

On Wednesday afternoon, Calero glanced at the Rolex watch on his wrist and thought that this would be one funeral he'd be early for. Adjusting the small white rose in the lapel of his beautifully tailored black jacket, he told himself that he felt okay. He had a job to do and he was going to do it looking right. Old Sarah had loved style and he didn't want to let her down on this special day.

He slipped quietly into the office and waited for the anticipated reaction. He got it. "Jesus H. Christ, you look like a Spanish Johnny Cash in that go-to-funeral outfit. When did you get those duds? Oh, no! Another pair of Tony Lama boots!" Olga glared at him.

"Can't wear brown boots with a black coat…and it wouldn't be respectful not to wear black." Calero smiled and winked at Mary.

"But a waistcoat! That thing was tailor-made on short notice, and I'll bet it cost a trailer-load of wheat for sure." Olga paused, softening a bit, and rolled her eyes toward heaven. "The white tie and white rose are a nice touch, though, I'll give you that."

Calero laughed. "Good to see you're back to normal, Olga. I like your femi-Nazi side better. You ever thought of being a cop?"

"I am a cop, Mr. Keen-Observer...I don't need to become one. Say, how're we going to pay for all that splendor? Sell the pregnant heifers...get you a job singing in a bar? Mary, hand him that old guitar over there. Might as well complete the picture."

"I have to go. I'll see you ladies later. I want to be early for Sarah and Miss Julie," Calero tossed over his shoulder as he went out the door.

"Hey, Johnny Cash, you forgot your guitar! Oh, and one more thing," Olga said, going quickly to the door and calling after him, "say a little prayer for me, too, Joe."

As he whizzed along the highway in the now spotless white truck, Calero felt alive and good inside. Maybe he couldn't afford the new clothes, but it would work out. It always worked out.

"What the...?" Calero smashed on the brakes and hit the side of the road in a broad skid before the two strangers out in his hay field knew what was happening. The dust cloud the skid created rolled over the men and their own truck. Coughing, they rubbed their eyes, and the next thing they saw was a man right out of the Old West—black hat, black boots, and a Winchester hanging from his left hand.

One of the men, big and very fat, found his tongue first and would later be sorry for it. "Well, if it isn't Matt Dillon!

Or is it Johnny Cash come to sing us a song while we work? Hey, Jerry, he gonna sing us a song."

"No...o...o, I'm gonna blow the pants off your fat ass unless you can reload that truck and then drive that trespassin' old wreck out my posted gate in five minutes...or less."

"You can't do much with the BB gun, Fancy Pants, and besides there's two of us. We could tear a lot of holes in that suit. You dig? Keep throwing that shit off the truck, Jerry."

As the man moved forward, the urge to hit and hit hard almost overwhelmed Calero, but he stayed calm. "Good point about the suit, you lumbering piece of *toro mierda.* You shit-dumping pigs just don't know your limitations, do you?" Calero pumped a round into the Winchester's chamber and the fat man's mouth fell open, his face turning to parchment. His partner Jerry began to run.

Feet spread in the dust, Calero carefully brought the weapon to his shoulder and squeezed off a shot. The fat man's shout of relief was followed by a long hiss as the front tire on the men's truck flattened. Calero ejected the shell, carefully picked it up, wrapped it in his handkerchief and placed it in his pocket. Without a word, he lowered the gun, spun around, and returned to his waiting truck. Shoving the rifle back into its scabbard, he lifted the cellular phone and dialed.

Moments later, with the truck door open, Calero leaned halfway out of the cab. He flicked the phone to its public address mode and began speaking. "You are both under arrest for trespassing. You may not leave the scene or remove the truck until the sheriff arrives. If you do, you will not only be charged with trespass and willful littering but with resisting arrest and leaving the scene of a crime, as well. You dig?" Then he slammed the truck door and drove off. Through the rear window he could see the two men frantically gathering up the trash they had dumped in his field.

"Please don't start the funeral without me, Miss Julie," Calero was whispering as he tore down the highway. Then the truck's phone rang and he answered it.

"Yeah, Sheriff, I called 911 and told them I had a little problem. There's some trash dumpers out here who need to be written up 'cause they're just dying to pay the county one thousand dollars for dumping crap on my property—probably for the umpteenth time. Recognized my voice huh, Sheriff? Yep, it's Calero, and I caught the bastards and arrested them. No, I can't wait for you to get here...I'm already late for a funeral. Those bums can't go far because they've got a flat left-front tire and no spare. Oh, and Sheriff, how soon do I get the five hundred dollar reward for catching them? Got a pair of boots need payin' for."

Calero swung off Highway 101 onto De La Cruz Boulevard and drove with intensity. He wanted to be there for Miss Sarah's funeral. She'd always been kind to him and she really had no one, except her sister, Miss Julie. He drove onto the mission grounds at the University of Santa Clara. This was the oldest university on the West Coast—a place he knew and loved. He saw a black hearse and cars lined up. He was on time.

He stopped at the guard house and the man told him to park over in front of the de Saisset Museum. Calero had visited the campus many times to study the old Spanish land grants and enjoy the art collection in the lovely little museum. He particularly liked the small bronze statue of a bull lost in a cape wound around the legs of a matador. He always thought of *Grande Padre Mustachio* when he touched it.

The statue was on loan from the Davis family—Miss Julie's family. He and Miss Sarah had talked about the statue many times. She loved it, too. The artist was unknown, but the work appeared to be very old. One fascinating aspect of it was that if you looked at the matador closely, you suspected the matador was a woman.

With a sigh, Calero parked and walked solemnly toward the church. There was much sadness in his heart, but he was glad he was here. As soon as he entered the side door of the old chapel, he knew this was not the old lady's funeral. There were too few mourners and only a scattering of priests—the chapel was half empty.

He hurried back to his truck and drove quickly to the nearby Catholic cemetery, hoping he would at least be on time for the private internment. He was, for Miss Julie had honored her sister's final request—one last drive past the old house where the two women had been born.

The house still stood on ten acres in the center of the city of Santa Clara. It was now worth an enormous amount of money, but they hadn't kept it for that reason. They kept it because it had been their home, the place where they were raised—in a grander time, in a grand but fading style.

Reaching the Jesuit cemetery, Calero walked over to the sisters' family plot. Seeing the freshly prepared grave, he murmured, "Good. No one here yet." The grave lay empty; Sarah still hadn't reached her final resting place. Calero stood there patiently waiting for the procession to arrive.

Looking off across the cemetery, he wondered about all the souls who had gone before him. Sisters and fathers, parishioners and children, all Catholics lying together in peace. Most had been given the final rites, just as Miss Sarah had. Many had put their affairs in order, as he knew she would have done.

Hearing the crunching of gravel, Calero turned and saw the hearse. It was followed by a limousine, then an old brown pickup and a battered Chevy moving slowly down the road toward him. He knew Domingo and a couple of the workers who had helped the sisters over the years would be in the pickup. Two Mexican families were crammed into the Chevy. That was all there was to the private funeral procession.

Domingo and three of the Mexican men removed the casket from the hearse and carried it reverently toward the grave site. Stepping out of the limousine was a tiny, frail woman dressed in black. It was Miss Julie. In a moment, a priest was hurrying to her side. A black veil covered Miss Julie's sparse grey hair and her lined face, but when she saw Calero, she lifted the veil and gave him a broad smile. "Thank you for coming, *Don* Calero. Thank you for coming." She left the priest and took Calero's arm. Walking to the edge of the grave where a few chairs had been placed, they sat down. As he held her hand, she sighed. "We were such good friends, Joe, such good friends. All these years and now it ends."

An elderly priest, one who had known the two sisters for many years, began the brief service. Everything he had to say had already been said in the chapel at Santa Clara. Now his words were only to commend Miss Sarah's soul to heaven and her body to the earth.

The priests at Santa Clara would mention her in their prayers for many months to come. The new performing arts theatre would be named after the two sisters who had funded it. And this was not the first money they had provided for Santa Clara education, for the university in general, and for the fathers. And it would not be the last.

So the fathers would remember her in their prayers, and someday students would ask who the theatre had been named after, but most would shrug and perhaps none would remember why it was called The Two Sisters Performing Arts Theatre.

Calero knew he would miss Miss Sarah. She had been good to him and he had been good to her. They always honored their contracts with one another. Nothing ever in writing.

He would farm the land, pay the rent, and give her a fair share of the crop, and often he had protected her from those who would take advantage of her.

Miss Sarah had been a good businesswoman. The frail woman whose hand he held would not get along so well now without her sister. Miss Julie could be in for some difficult times. Miss Sarah and Miss Julie had been twins, but the old lady was born first and she was strong, a leader. Miss Julie followed later and she was a frail, easily frightened woman who needed support.

So, Calero had come to honor both the sisters, to please Miss Sarah in death by holding her sister Julie's hand, by being there. Domingo and the others stood off to one side, holding their hats and staring down at the ground.

When the priest finished his remarks, Domingo led the few mourners up to Miss Julie and bowed. Only Domingo shook her hand. Then he bent down, took a handful of earth and gently sprinkled it on the coffin. Turning, he walked slowly back to the pickup, his hat still in his hand. His two workers followed close behind, holding their hats, their heads bowed.

Calero rose then and walked to the grave. Picking up a handful of earth, his eyes filled with tears. Gently, he dropped the earth upon the coffin, the dirt and stones rumbling a last good-bye. As a final gesture he removed the white rose from his lapel, dropped it in the grave, and watched as it came to rest on the coffin. Then he walked away to compose himself, leaving Miss Julie alone for a few minutes.

Then she came to him and said, "Please come to the car, Joe. I need to talk with you." He walked with her to the limousine, and once they were inside, she pressed an electric button that slid a glass partition into place, guaranteeing their privacy. They sat in silence for a time before Miss Julie spoke.

"Well, it is done. I'm all alone now. Thank you for being here, Joe. My sister cared a great deal for you, and I'm glad. You were the son she or I never had. She has left you some gifts, Joe, and you must accept them...without question...without protest. It's all in these papers...you can read them later." Miss Julie handed Calero a thick manila envelope. "All that is required of you is that you stand by me and help me. We both knew I would need someone and we chose you."

Calero sat silent, all protests hidden behind his reassuring, yet deeply concerned face.

"And now, Joe, a very personal gift for you from my sister." Reaching down by her feet, Miss Julie picked up a heavy package and set it between them on the seat. "Please open it now. It's yours," she said as she patted the box.

Silently, he closely examined the twenty-by-six-inch carton. It was labeled with his name. Then, with shock, he knew what would be inside. His hands began to sweat as he painstakingly opened the box and then lifted the bronze statue of the matador and the bull out of its blue velvet resting place.

The image of *Grande Padre Mustachio* flooded his mind and again he heard the music of the *corrida*. Bringing the statue up to his face, he pressed it to his check, and his tears for a much beloved grandfather dripped on the bronze.

"Thank you so much, so very much." Calero's voice was barely audible, but Miss Julie could feel the words.

7

Olga Plays Detective

"Don't cry for me, Buenos Aires...," Olga sang and hummed her personal version of the hit song from the musical *Evita* as she moved about the office. She had come in early as usual, but this morning she had "unauthorized" work, as she called it, to get out of the way before Mary showed up.

Calero had left shortly after dawn to investigate a mystery—his dog was missing. The note in Olga's hand said that Calero and Domingo had launched a search on horseback at first light.

The dog would be fine, she thought. He was always chasing some animal off the ranch, later returning with assorted cuts and scrapes. As long as he stayed away from the runaway black stallion that had almost killed him as a pup, he'd live. Spooky was a lot like Calero, she thought; intelligent, but always toying with danger.

For the past two weeks, Spooky had been shut in the barn to keep him off Sinnobar Hill. Olga and Calero hoped to lure the poachers closer, and their plan seemed to be working. Calero had heard Spooky's people-bark three nights in the last two weeks, and just a couple of nights ago, he'd dragged Spooky inside the house to shut him up.

Olga's thoughts returned to her native country again. "Ah, Argentina, how I miss you and the old life," she whispered to herself. She ran the *Evita* cassette back, playing the song again and singing even louder. "Don't cry for me, Buenos Aires, the truth is I never left you…"

She always became misty-eyed on hearing the song. It reminded her of the old days when the Perons were in power and her family was a part of it all. But, that was all over now, she had a new life. I wish you could see me now, Papa and Mama. Life is good here and Calero—well, he is the best…you would love him, too.

It felt wonderful to be part of Rancho Calero, and she loved the fact she now had a clandestine mission as well. An old friend, Newell, an undercover agent, knew of her past work and trusted her completely. He was aware she knew how to get certain things done without arousing suspicion, without getting caught, and now she was involved in something very big and it thrilled her.

Newell—called that because he hated his first name, Orvil—had been an agent with the Federal Bureau of Investigation for the last twenty years. She had become friends with him during her FBI-assisted relocation fifteen years ago. He kept in touch both officially and as a friend who cared.

When she had called his San Francisco headquarters to ask if she could borrow an infrared camera, he told her, strictly off the record, that he was doing a bit of work in Sinnobar Hills. They had arranged to meet behind the coffee shop in town, and Olga knew it would be a very interesting meeting.

Mary's arrival at the office freed Olga to make the drive into town. Arriving at the Sinnobar Hills Coffee Shop, she parked her car and walked down the alley to the back of the shop. She was right on time, but where was Newell? Moments later, a youngish Mexican boy bicycled up to her and asked, "You Miss Olga?"

When she nodded, he smiled, moved conspiratorially close, and said, *"Bueno!* A black man, in a black suit, in a black car...he said to meet him behind the post office right away." Then he pedaled off and didn't look back.

"Well, shit, and I just put a quarter in the parking meter." Olga frowned, returned to her car, and drove quickly to the back of the post office.

She found Newell in the back row of cars parked there and her heart quickened. He was leaning against the side of his car and hadn't seen her yet. She parked unnoticed and slipped up on him.

"Hey, you!" she said, faking it in her best male voice, and watched as Newell spun around, his hand going under the back of his coat.

"Gotcha!" Olga gloated happily.

"Jesus! Don't ever do that—especially in this town, de Grut!"

"Just a concerned citizen helping to keep our FBI alert," Olga said with a broad smile. "Besides, you owe me a quarter. Furthermore, if your cover is to look like an IBM salesman, I can tell you it isn't working. Everything about your get-up spells cop. But where's the trench coat?"

"I'm not supposed to be undercover. That's why I need you."

"You need me? I need you and your camera. I aim to catch me a poacher."

"Oh, right. I got that for you," Newell said, and moved around to the trunk and opened it.

Olga whistled as she peered inside. "Wish I'd had that kind of stuff when I was in Argentina."

"Most of it is so new it would blow your mind," Newell said, and handed her a black canvas bag. "State-of-the-art video camera, time-lapse device, remote control trigger transmitter with a three-mile range, and more. And if someone steals that camera, we can locate it by satellite. Oh, and get this…the camera has a human-sensor trigger that starts the camera rolling when a suspect is within fifty yards of the scene."

Newell closed the trunk, and as Olga let out a low whistle, he warned her, "Lose this stuff and it will cost me a year's salary and my job."

"This is wonderful, Newell. But now," and he heard the serious concern in her voice, "how can I help you?"

"We have to hurry this up, Olga. We shouldn't be seen together today or any other time in the near future. I can't tell you much, other than it involves Sinnobar Bank and Trust. The guy running that bank is a chronic bender of federal law.

"That's why I'm here, but the power in this city thinks I'm here on duty rotation. What I need from you is to nose around…you'll hear things, spoken in Spanish, that may be useful. Nobody in the Latino community would believe a Nordic-looking chick like you would understand Spanish.

"I need a break in this case, Olga. See if you can get close to some of the people who do cleaning jobs. They're almost all Mexicans and many are illegals…exploited by the bank and other businesses. Maybe we can hire one of them to feed us information on phone calls, key bank customers…the usual."

Olga nodded eagerly. "My pleasure. First, I'll listen around, then I'll…"

"Spare me the details, Olga. I know you know how to do what and when. And, by the way, don't call me on the Rancho Calero phone, and don't call me at the San Francisco office. I want you to use the number on this card. Now, commit this to memory—the first three digits of the phone number are wrong. Replace them with nines, and you'll reach me."

Newell took Olga's hand then and, looking deeply into her eyes, said, "Please be very careful. These suspects can be ruthless." Then, without another word, he quickly got in his car and drove away. Olga entered the post office to buy a sheet of Elvis stamps for Mary.

On her return to the ranch, Olga hid the special camera in a little-used file drawer, intending to exclude Mary from the secret. But later that same day she found that Mary, as usual, missed very little. Coming quietly and unexpectedly into the office, Olga heard Mary talking to Calero in a whispered voice. "Better take a look at what Miss Olga has hidden in the back of the file drawer over there."

"What is it, Mary?" Calero had asked. "A German porno magazine?"

"Oh, no," Mary had answered, her face turning red. "I think it's a spy camera. There's a manual, too. I looked at it, and it's heavy stuff on how to catch criminals, Mr. Calero. Mum's the word, though. I bet I'm not supposed to know about it, but I thought you should know."

Both Calero and the girl turned as they realized Olga had entered the office. Mary, more red-faced than ever, muttering something about needing to go to the kitchen, scurried out of the room.

As for Calero, he matter-of-factly asked, "When do we set up that equipment to catch the poachers, Olga?"

She showed her surprise. "Darn you, Calero, how'd you know about that?"

"It's my business to know, spy-lady," Calero said. Going out on the porch, he called to Domingo down at the stable to saddle two horses. "Buck for me, and a nice calm one for Olga," he yelled. Returning to the office, he said, "Get that stuff out of the file, Olga. We're going to catch us some poachers."

Within minutes they were riding up Sinnobar Hill, the black bag containing the infrared camera securely slung over

Olga's shoulder. Two hours later, on their return, Calero went to his bedroom and set the remote tripping device for the camera next to his alarm clock.

Now all was ready. They had hidden the camera well, but so strategically placed that anyone reaching the top of the hill would automatically trigger the camera. And Calero could use the remote device to trigger the camera from his bed. He liked that.

8

The Camera Plays Detective

The thunder of swiftly racing hooves broke into Olga's reverie. Startled, she looked out the office window in time to see Domingo and Calero gallop across the yard and skid to a halt at the hitching rail. Calero was on the ground and walking rapidly toward the office before the Buck had fully stopped.

The black camera bag firmly clutched in his hand, he was calling to her, "Olga! Olga! We've got to get this film into the VCR...And Spooky's been kidnapped!"

Calero rushed into the family room, just down the hall from the office, and was quickly followed by Olga. Domingo pushed through the door after them.

"You take the phones, Mary," Olga bellowed unceremoniously down the hall to the girl, and then turned back to the two men. "And you, Calero, give me that camera...and the details of what you and Domingo uncovered."

Calero handed the case to Olga. "Well, I heard Spooky's barking around four this morning, then it suddenly stopped. That's when Domingo discovered Spooky had made his escape from the barn. Looks like he clawed his way up the ladder to the loft—you've seen how he does that—and leaped out the upper door."

"Christ, that's a fifteen-foot drop," Olga said.

"I guess he wanted those *hombres* bad and went after them," Domingo said, and looked grim. "The dog's hurt—

we found blood. But not just his blood. Someone has a piece missing. Perhaps our Spooky tried to tear him a new *atras*." Domingo smiled at the thought.

"*Atras?* What's that mean?" Mary asked from where she stood in the doorway.

"Asshole, Mary. It means that Spooky may have tried to tear him a new asshole. And you're supposed to be tending the phones," Olga responded, annoyance in her voice.

"I can hear the phones just fine from here, Miss Olga, and I'm a part of this, too. You can't leave me out!" And she shoved her hands resolutely into the pockets of her stone-washed jeans.

Olga scowled but decided to let her stay, and Calero continued his story, "It was only a few minutes later when we rode out of here fast and headed up Sinnobar Hill...but we must have just missed the sons of bitches. Domingo and I rode around the clearing where we'd set up the infrared camera, being careful not to mess up any tracks they may have left. Then we walked down the other side, hoping to intercept them at the road. We didn't.

"But listen to this. We'd left the horses tethered near the clearing, and old eagle-eye Domingo leads the way back to the top of the hill but insists we stay off the beaten path. Good move, because when it gets even lighter, what do you think we find?"

"What?" Mary and Olga both cried out in unison.

"Evidence. Graphic evidence. Tracks everywhere and signs of a struggle. Spooky's paw prints with blood in them, and a man's footprints walking backward dragging something—probably Spooky's body. Also, there was quite a bit of blood dribbled alongside the drag marks. We think that blood came from the person walking beside the one dragging the dog."

"And, there was a third *hombre*. Different shoe bottoms," Domingo added. "First, I think the three men kill the dog, but then I think no. The man knock Spooky out and carried him away. We could find no body or no grave. I think the *hombres* wish us to believe the dog has run away."

"And when we were walking all over the hill," Calero added, "I felt something odd through the soles of my boots. It didn't seem to feel like the rest of the terrain. It was more gritty, coarser. When I stooped to gather up a handful of it, I accidentally moved a little rock, and there it was—a hole the diameter of a quarter, going straight down."

"They made other holes, too. We found more they tried to cover up," Domingo said.

Lowering his voice, Calero said, "Now get this, ladies…then forget you ever heard it. I'm about to tell you the secret of all secrets. When the sun was full up, I held up a handful of that gritty stuff and watched as the wind blew it from my hand. All I can say is, it wasn't sinnobar, and it wasn't silver."

"Gold!" Mary gasped, and then covered her mouth with both hands. She didn't want anyone sending her from the room.

Calero said softly, "Patience. Patience. You'll learn in good time, Mary."

"Now it's time to roll that video." Calero's voice had returned to its normal level. "Let's see what those bastards look like."

They all watched avidly as time-lapse images began to appear on the TV screen. Digital dates were sharply indicated on each one. Apparently, on three separate occasions, two men had come up the trail. It looked like they carried hooded lights that only reflected downward and lit a small patch of ground. The men rarely spoke and then only in muffled voices. There was the sound of a case clicking open as a tool was removed. Then a whine. The men were drilling!

"So that's what I've been hearing. Kept thinking I was having a nightmare about that kid and the jet-ski that time." Calero paused, then explained to the other viewers, "That's a high-powered, battery-driven drill they're using."

The frantic barking of a dog could now be heard, even over the sound of the drilling, and then Spooky streaked into the picture on the TV screen. Everyone cheered as Spooky charged the man bent over the drill. In a moment, the man screamed and straightened up. Spooky's teeth had sunk into the man's rear end.

"There's the new asshole!" Olga whooped.

Another man, a fat one, moved in swiftly then and jabbed what appeared to be a hypodermic needle into Spooky's flank. Suddenly the dog went limp and slumped to the ground, and the man he had bitten began viciously kicking him. The watchers in the room moaned with each kick, and Calero leaped to his feet and screamed, "You bastard! I'll kill you for that!"

The fat man began dragging Spooky away while the bitten man wiped at his bloody hip. He stared at his blood-covered hand and then rushed at Spooky to kick him again, but the fat man jumped in front of him and yelled sharply, *"Alto! Alto, ahora!"*

"The *gordo hombre* is *Mexicano*," Domingo commented, "but the other two are *gringos*."

"I pity those guys when Spooky wakes up. I know they'll get no mercy from me," Calero hissed, and he turned the machine off as the film ended.

Olga felt terrible. She was sure the dog was dead but knew Calero needed to believe his Spooky was alive. He needed that illusion to blanket his pain. But she also knew they should waste no time. "Well, we went fishing for minnows and landed a shark, and by the smell of things, we must be onto something big—thanks to Spooky and to Newell's infrared camera. So, next thing I do is get this film to Newell and have him get us some crucial blow-ups. Hopefully, we can even get some clear I.D.'s. And we need the lettering enlarged on that drill case—maybe there's a company name we can use." Then, as a telephone shrilled back in the office, "Get that phone, Mary!"

"Yes, ma'am," Mary replied, and hurried off to the office to pick up the phone. She listened a moment, then said, "Oh, Miss Rodriguez. Just a moment, please." Mary pushed the hold button before calling down the hall, "It's that Rodriguez woman, Mr. Calero. Want to talk to her?"

"Sure do," Calero answered brightly, and moved quickly to the office.

"Miss Gag-Me…reeling in the vulnerable," Olga said to Domingo, making a gagging gesture with her finger.

"The dark beauty he calls Nola? The rich one with the stallion, the one who makes pets out of cows? She will put a ring in Calero's nose and turn him into a steer. He can't handle that one. I watch, and I see many bad signs, Olga. We must find him another woman quick before he ends up fighting for his life in the wrong arena."

"Hell, Domingo, I've picked the right woman for him. You know…that college gal who raises Spanish bulls. She's a real looker, but she's smart and down to earth, too. No flashy clothes and fast car. God, I can't stand to see that Nola in those 'come-fuck-me' high-heel custom boots…But Calero is thinking with his gonads. I think he's hooked already."

"No. Not quite yet. If hooked, he would already be looking around for a place to die. But he is still at play…that's why we have a chance. This Nola woman is one from the past, and here she is again to destroy everything…everything…one more time." Domingo mumbled and shook his head as he walked toward the office.

Olga followed him into the office and glared at Calero, who was still on the phone. Calero's face turned red and he murmured, "Just a moment, Nola, I'll take the call upstairs." Putting her on hold, he left the office without another word.

Mary and Olga both stared at the tiny glowing light that indicated the phone was busy an interminably long time. It wasn't like Calero to spend a long time on the phone, but when Nola called, time didn't seem to exist.

"Olga, what do men see in women like her? I know she has a great figure, pretty face and all, but it's so obvious she just wants one thing from him."

"What one thing, Mary?"

"You know…sex."

"Oh, that. Mary, men will kill for that, and if they think they are about to get it, and then don't get it, watch out! They'll kill the one they desire…or themselves. They'll even get married just to get a lay. And that Mr. Big *Cojones* upstairs is going to end up in major trouble unless we hook him up with…"

"Karin Noble," Mary interrupted. "That's the woman for Mr. Calero. I thought they were about to be an item until that Nola came along. Hey, by the way, did you see Karin's picture in the *Farm Journal?*" Mary jumped up and rescued a magazine from a pile on the floor. "What a great picture, standing there with her winning bull. Mr. Calero's just got to fall for her, or I swear I'll never understand."

"Never understand?" Olga questioned.

"I'll never understand what it's all about, Olga."

9

A Multimillion-dollar Signature

Calero realized it was barely daylight as he reached to pick up the ringing telephone.

"Joe, I've done a very bad thing," the elderly, brittle voice whispered into Calero's ear. "I signed a paper I didn't read, and now the Santa Clara homestead is gone forever, just like my sister."

Calero heard a little sob before Miss Julie went on. "Joe, how could I be so foolish? But I trusted him…and now this. I should have called you first but I didn't want to bother you, and now the land and the house are gone—gone in the scribble of a signature."

"I know you're in a lot of pain right now, Miss Julie, but no one is taking your home away from you while I'm still breathing!"

"But, I signed! I signed," she said through her tears.

"Miss Julie, listen to me." Calero shifted the receiver to his other ear and grabbed pen and paper. "Who did this to you, and just what did you sign?"

"George Farley, a dear friend. Always came for coffee and sat and talked. He made a lonely old fool feel good. My sister said he was the only honest real estate man she had ever met. Farley Real Estate Company has been around for a hundred years. Mr. Farley's a rich man in his own right. Why would he do this to me, Joe?"

"Again, Miss Julie, what did you sign and when did you sign it?" Calero asked in an attempt to keep her focused.

"Well, two weeks ago I signed a contract to just have the property appraised—or so I thought. Then someone from the escrow company called yesterday and said the property had been bought by an out-of-town corporation for three million dollars cash. I couldn't believe it. The woman said there was no mistake—my offer to sell and their acceptance and check for three million were on her desk."

Calero covered the mouth piece as he hissed, "Shit!" Then he wrote down the name of George Farley and the figure three million dollars.

"I'm sorry to call you so early, Joe, but I didn't sleep all night and wanted to reach you before you went anywhere this morning. I can't face this alone." More tears.

"You did right, Julie." Calero realized, even as he said it, that this was the first time he had not called her Miss Julie. "Tell me this? What would it look like if it were the way you wanted it to be? That is, Julie, how do you want all this to turn out?"

"Oh, Joe, I just want the house back. They can have the land even though it's worth a lot more—but not my home. Never, Joe, never my home!"

Calero liked the surge of spirit from the usually shy and frail old woman. Julie might be coming into her own—but could she maintain it through the fight that had to lie ahead? It would be a fight they probably couldn't win, unless she were declared incompetent, and he wouldn't do that to her. There had to be another way.

"Julie, can I have your word that from now on we work together on this...and all your business matters?"

"Yes, Joe, you have my word. But I want to pay you for this. I'll pay you whatever you wish."

"Now, Julie, as only you and I know, I have already been paid, and paid well. But we do have a fight ahead and we'll have to work together to lure this thieving bull close enough to win back what is rightfully yours. Do you have George Farley's telephone number?"

"I have both his work and his unlisted home phone. He said never to give his home number to anyone, but I guess I don't owe him any courtesy now."

"Right, Julie." Calero began to see images in his mind. "Never forget an animal is an animal. If a matador feels sorry for a bull and begins to believe the bull will always make an honest pass, he will soon take a horn. That animal Farley stuck it to you, and we're going to have our moment of truth."

"What? I don't understand what you're saying." Julie sounded bewildered.

"That's okay, Julie." Calero realized what he had done. "I was just thinking out loud. Now, let me have Farley's numbers, please."

When she had given him the telephone numbers, he told her, "You get some rest now, Miss Julie, and let me start to work on this for you."

After he had hung up the phone, Calero rolled over and glanced at the clock. It was 5:15 A.M. He rose and dressed quickly as a plan began to take shape in his mind. He walked over to the gun cabinet and took out a small derringer, loaded it, and slipped it into the custom-made holster on the outside of his left boot—butt end out. He dropped his black trouser leg over the gun and checked in the mirror for the slight bulge it made. It would do.

The office was a mess when he entered. Olga had been off for a few days and neatness had gone out the door with her. He had intended to straighten it up this morning before she came in, so as to avoid the harangue that only she could deliver. He sat at his desk and dialed George Farley's unlisted home number.

"Farley, here," a sleepy voice answered after the sixth ring.

"Good morning, Mr. George Farley. This is Dial-A-Prayer. We have been asked to pray for you, in this, your hour of need. Do you have a favorite prayer or should we choose something suitable?"

"What the hell are you talking about, and why are you calling me so damned early in the morning?"

"It's never too early for prayers, George Farley, and you are going to need lots of them. For starters, you could pray that the papers you got Julie Davis to sign find their way out of the escrow office and back into Miss Julie's innocent hands. Amen. Praise the Lord! Can you say 'Amen, praise the Lord'? Repeat after me. Are you ready?"

"I'll tell you what I'm ready to do, you nut case," Farley snapped in his now wide-awake voice. "I'm ready to terminate this nonsense. How the devil did you get this number?"

"The Lord works in mysterious ways, my wayward brother. But there is hope of salvation for you and your real estate firm. However, the hand of judgment will lay heavy upon the thief who does not repent. And one way or the other, you are going to repent. Amen. Praise the Lord!"

"Who are you calling a thief?" Farley's voice had raised an octave.

"Take the first step toward salvation, George Farley, and return the papers NOW!"

Calero heard the receiver bang down on the other end of the line, and jerked the phone away from his ear. A smile crept across his face as he placed the receiver of his own phone back in its cradle.

"Saving this sinner may take a little time and a personal visit," he mused aloud.

"And since when did you join the ranks of the saved?" Olga asked, continuing to lean against the door frame that had been her support for several minutes.

"Oh! When did you come in?"

"Right at the beginning of the service, Reverend. Sounds like you've started a new business. Dial-A-Prayer? Give me a break. I'm gone three days, you get religion, and the office has turned into a gypsy garbage dump. I won't have my office looking like this. Jesus H. Christ, it's as big a mess as when I first took over. This mansion is an historical monument and deserves neatness. Neatness!" Olga yelled.

Calero watched as she stormed around the office, doing what he called "her German neatness thing."

"Welcome back, Olga. How about a little kiss...or perhaps a prayer?"

"Don't fuck with me, Calero. I've been under a lot of pressure these last few days. The Historical Society will be here at eight o'clock, and the Save Rancho Calero Committee will meet here at nine."

"I'd help, Olga, but I have a prayer meeting with one of my fallen brothers and can't be late."

"Get out! Out!"

Calero scurried out the door and headed quickly toward his truck. He wanted to beat Farley to the draw, and to do that, he needed the element of surprise.

With Olga back, he knew the ranch would run smoothly. She'd received a lot of support from the Sinnobar Hills Historical Society but very little money. They had the money, but it seemed some possible big donors weren't in favor of the restoration project.

That was no problem for Olga. First, she had built a list of the one hundred and eighty boarders at the ranch that showed their skills, services and connections. Then she had formed ten restoration committees with eight members each. Each of these cells, as she called them, elected a captain who reported personally to Olga. They were all fond of her and they feared her disapproval.

She was a general of a woman. Each time the Historical Society held a meeting at the ranch to discuss what needed to be done, they could only collectively gasp. Either a project was already done or well underway.

But what else was it Olga had said about a meeting of the...what was it...the Save Rancho Calero Committee? That was a new one, but it would have to wait until later.

Farley Real Estate Company loomed into view ahead of him, and Calero cursed as he saw that a woman was just going into the office. He parked his truck nearby and then walked past the real estate company's door. The woman inside bustled around and then left the room.

Calero tried the door and found it open. Slipping in, he walked straight through a sea of desks and saw a door with the sign George Farley, President. Opening the door, he slipped inside and exhaled loudly. Now he pulled a comfortable leather chair to a place just behind the door. Then he sat down and waited. But not for long.

The door opened, and it was George Farley who stepped inside. He kicked the door shut with his foot and then hurried to his desk. Sitting down heavily, he picked up the telephone and dialed. It was while he waited for his call to be answered that he looked up and saw Calero. Slowly he lowered the phone receiver to its base and sucked air in between his teeth.

Calero stood, and pulled his chair sideways so that it blocked the office door. Then he sat down again and slowly and deliberately crossed his legs. Farley's eyes focused on the derringer peeking out from beneath Calero's left trouser leg.

"Just who the hell are you, and how did you get into my office?" Farley demanded.

"First things first," Calero answered. "You know very well who I am. Don't ever hang up on me again unless you want to meet me unexpectedly...around any corner, at any hour. You are mine…until they either drag you from the arena or you retire."

"What on earth are you talking about? When did I hang up on you? When did I even talk to you?" Farley's questions came nervously. "Why are you threatening me?"

"Around any corner, any hour," Calero repeated in a low, menacing tone.

Farley's forehead beaded with a nervous shine. He mopped at it with his handkerchief and frowned as he stared anxiously at his accuser. Calero, beginning to realize what a weak character he was confronting, came right out then, accusing Farley of lying about Miss Julie's land deal.

"I only did what she wanted," Farley offered helplessly, denying any wrongdoing. "It's out of my hands—it's a done deal. Finished! Sinnobar Title Company has the offer to sell, the acceptance papers, and the check."

Calero scratched his chin, changed his position in the chair, and then leaned toward Farley. "The only thing that makes sense here is…," and he paused for effect, "that somebody owns you, George Farley. How's that sound for a guess?"

Color drained from Farley's face and he, too, changed his sitting position. Mr. Keen-Observer Calero knew he had hit pay dirt and dug a little deeper. "I'm going to find out who owns you, Farley, but it may be too late for you by then. I'll do one thing for you, though. I'll visit you in prison and I will say a prayer for you."

Farley stared silently and again mopped his forehead with his now damp handkerchief. Calero rose from his chair, moved it aside, and opened the office door a crack. Then he turned, raised his right hand and said in a pontifical manner, "Amen, brother. Praise the Lord." Then he was gone.

As Calero closed Farley's door behind him, he saw that Farley's secretary was now at her desk. Looking up, she asked,

"When did you come in? I didn't know Mr. Farley had an early appointment."

"Oh, didn't you see me walk right by your desk?" Calero said in his most innocent voice.

At that moment, the sound of retching could be heard coming from Farley's office, and both Calero and the secretary turned toward it. "Maybe he's swallowed something he can't keep down," Calero said with convincing concern. He bowed, put on his hat and walked out. Once in the street, he headed for the Sinnobar Title Company.

Once there, he took a quick audit of the situation. "Morning, ma'am," Calero said, tipping his hat to the woman at the front desk. Attractive woman, midthirties, no wedding band, picture of three kids. Her nameplate read June Jeffrey. "I represent Miss Julie Davis and would like to ask you a few questions about the escrow on her Santa Clara property."

"Do you have any identification?"

"Sure do," he said, and pulled a Rancho Calero Stables card out of his pocket and handed it to her. "Joe Calero, at your service."

"Oh, you must own the stable my kids have been bugging me about. You give rides and lessons out there, don't you?"

"Sure do, and if those three nice-looking kids in the picture are yours, I'd say they're ready to ride. Let me have that card back a minute and I'll bring even bigger smiles to their faces than in that picture there."

Calero took the card and wrote "Three free lessons" and signed his name. Sliding it back across the desk, he said, "Now, I know Miss Julie stands to receive a three million dollar check that you're holding, but what if she's changed her mind and doesn't want to sell?"

"Look. Thanks for the lessons, but I can't discuss this with you without an okay from the principals. Please understand I would like to, but I can't. What I can do is answer general questions about how escrows work, how they are opened, how they are closed…"

"How they are delayed?" Calero interrupted, smiling warmly.

"Yes, and how they are delayed. A dispute can delay one, someone refuses to sign off, things like that."

"I'll bet you've seen some real messes in your day."

"Boy, have I! One dragged on for a year and finally the court ordered the escrow closed."

"Ever had the court order an escrow set aside?" which is what Calero really wanted to know about.

"Yes, for fraud, but I couldn't tell you about that. It's confidential."

"But it did involve Farley Real Estate, I think the paper said."

"No—yes—well, I couldn't say anything about that. Maybe I'd better stop talking to you."

Bingo! Calero was elated. "You have been most kind, Mrs. Jeffrey. Or may I call you June? Come out for a ride soon. While the children take their lessons, perhaps you and I could take a ride together."

She blushed. "Thank you. I do want to be helpful," she said, with a hint of interest in her voice.

"The pleasure is all mine, June," he said, and as he turned and left, the woman's eyes followed him out the door.

Once in his truck he called Julie. "I've got great news, Julie. I can't go into the details now, but we are going to get that deal set aside. First, I want you to stay away from the title company. Don't return their calls. Have nothing to do with that thief Farley. This is not the first time he's done this, and we owe it to the world to take him out of the real estate business. In fact, we need you to be incommunicado. How about taking a trip for a couple of weeks?"

"Why, that sounds wonderful, Joe. I'd love to take a cruise to Mexico...I've always wanted to do that. But are you sure it's what I should do? And will two weeks be long enough?"

"Yes, I'm sure, and two weeks is just right. First, we retain an attorney and then you cruise while he and I go to work on this matter."

"Oh, Joe, I don't like attorneys. My sister used to say they were the only professionals licensed by the state to lie." They both laughed at the old joke.

"I know, Julie. It has to be the right attorney and one not owned by the town. I'll find him."

"Thank you, Joe. You are a love to help me. I trust you completely and will just follow your lead. But I feel very tired now. I'm going to shut off my phone and go to bed. I'm just so tired." Calero heard the soft click as she hung up the phone.

He worried about Miss Julie all the way back to the ranch. There was a lot of money involved, but Julie didn't need any more money. It certainly wasn't worth tiring her to death over. Was he doing the right thing—the best thing for her? Did the homestead really mean that much to her? Why was he doing it? Was it really for principle, or because it was another dangerous encounter in the arena of life, a challenge he couldn't resist? The smell of danger, the brush of the horn.

Would he have shot that bastard Farley today? The thing that made his heart pound now was the knowledge that he would have shot him in a flash if Farley had drawn on him. But Farley, the cornered bull he thought he would have to put down, turned out to be just another bad bull from a second-rate ranch. Farley would cave in, spill his guts, run away, and self-destruct. They would win if Julie had the strength for it...and if they got the right attorney.

Olga would know the right man, or would have the right contact. Now he couldn't wait to get back to the ranch and to Olga, that storm trooper of neatness.

10

A Matter of Honor

"Vat's dis?" Olga hissed the words in her best German accent as she held an invoice high over her head. Her back was to Calero as he entered the office, and the sight of her wide neck and her heavy shoulders beneath her black suit jacket made him flash back to some old World War II German movie he had seen. No wonder people either feared her or stood in awe of her. Calero did neither because he knew the truth. Olga was soft, kind and very gentle. He wondered if it bugged her to know he could see right through her.

"Damn it, you found the invoice for the gloves. Those were supposed to be a present for you, my sweet gentle one," he said, and he put his hands on her shoulders and gently massaged the tense muscles.

"*Toro mierda.* They're for Ms. Gag-Me—you know it and I know it." Then, relaxing a bit, she said, "I'll give you fifteen minutes to get your cheatin', two-timin' hands off my voluptuous shoulders. I've had a hell of a day already and it isn't over yet. A one hundred ninety-nine dollar pair of gloves for that woman! I just don't get it. She wear 'em during sex, or what?"

"Be nice, Olga. I'll buy a pair for you, too."

"Don't you dare. We can't afford this pair. Besides, I'd rather have a pair of claws so I could tear her eyes out."

Calero moved to his desk and spied the thirty thousand dollar check from A&X Computers. "Wow, you really got it!"

"Of course I got it. I said I'd rip them a new terminal and I did just that. They've owed us that money for over a year. We did the disking of their five hundred-acre site on time, and on budget. They won't be late with a payment again. I reminded them that we're not a bank! You should have been there, Calero."

Olga's face showed her pleasure as she recalled the encounter. "I marched through that lobby, then the finance department, and right into the vice-president's office like a blonde freight train. As luck would have it, the company president was sitting right there, too. I learned that a bit later when the VP tried to dismiss me. This soft voice broke in and asked, 'May I be helpful?' Well, I handed the man our bill, and he took a look at it. Then he frowned when he saw the due date, and he took out a pen and wrote across it 'Pay now.' Then he signed his name under that."

Calero was enjoying Olga's recital. "Then what happened?"

"The VP was sent to get the check, and this other guy, who turned out to be the president, and I had a nice talk. When the check came, I gave the president a couple of free ride passes—and left the VP with nothing but egg on his face. I just said, 'I presume that these little matters can be handled by mail in the future and in a timely manner?' Then the president said, 'You can count on it, Ms. de Grut.'"

"Great job, Olga. Great job. Now, on to something less positive. Miss Julie has been swindled into selling her birthplace. I want to stop the sale, and I have a plan, but it's going to take just the right attorney. He should be a man Julie will respect and like. Maybe someone closer to her age, lots of gray hair, a grandfather figure—a gentleman. And he needs to be from out of town, yet not seem like an outsider or one of those slick big-city types."

Calero frowned as Olga turned and picked up the phone. "Are you listening to me, Olga? Quit dialing that phone...I really need your help."

"Stop babbling, I'm getting you your attorney."

"You know already?"

"Of course," she said with a challenging look. Then, "Is this Judge Melbourne C. McPhearson's residence? Could I please speak with the judge? Oh, well could you have him call Ms. Olga de Grut? He has my number. Thank you." She hung up and turned to Calero.

"Now, Calero, suppose you give me all the details. Late afternoon tea should do the trick for a gentlewoman and a gentleman to meet. I know he'll take the case...and he'll win it for her. A gentleman like the judge could do nothing less. It would be a matter of honor."

It was three days later when Miss Julie and Calero were being whisked along the highway toward Los Gatos in Julie's old Mercedes limousine. The car was still immaculate, like new, and the ride was smooth, but both Calero and Miss Julie were on edge. Would the judge really take the case, as Olga had insisted he would?

The limousine rolled smoothly past the outskirts of Los Gatos and then the two stone cats that guarded the entrance to the judge's home loomed up at the side of the road. Miss Julie's chauffeur turned into the driveway where the double gates stood open, and as they passed through, the gates closed slowly behind them. There was no turning back now. Calero took Miss Julie's hand. It was going to be hard for him to ask for the judge's help, but he had to, for her sake.

The limousine wound up the steep wooded drive for a good mile before it rounded a bend and came to the house in all its elegant splendor. A true southern mansion with tall white pillars, expansive veranda, and a staircase that swept down to the circular drive. An assured elderly gentleman in a dark suit stood at the front door and greeted them. "Good afternoon. I'm Colonel McPhearson's butler. Welcome to Briarwood."

Calero helped Miss Julie from the car and escorted her up the stairs. The two stepped inside the large reception hall and stood for a moment, gazing up at the double sweeping staircase leading to the upper floors. Then the butler spoke again. "The colonel will be right down to greet you. Please follow me." A short distance down the hall, he opened two tall doors leading into a library and said, "Tea will be served in a moment. Please be comfortable." He left them then, quietly closing the library doors behind him.

"My, my, my. Very grand, indeed," Miss Julie said, slipping regally into a high-backed chair.

Calero felt totally out of place and didn't know where to sit. He was glad Olga had insisted he wear his go-to-funeral suit, but he still felt out of place.

Within minutes, the doors opened and Colonel McPhearson stepped into the room. He was a handsome man, well over six feet, with a trim body and an abundant head of white hair. "Miss Julie, what an honor to meet you. Thank you for being so kind as to visit me here at Briarwood." He took her hand and gently kissed the back of it. Then he turned to Calero, "And you, sir, must be *Don* Calero, from the great Spanish bullfighting family. Ms. de Grut speaks very highly of you. I must say, you have done marvelous things to the old Cash mansion." He shook Calero's hand firmly.

"Thank you for your kind words, Colonel. You've seen Rancho Calero then?"

"Indeed I have, and I applaud the results. You have a remarkable sense of history. I'm one of those who believe that if we don't preserve our history, we are doomed to back into the future." And then, as the library doors opened, "Ah, the tea is ready."

The butler began the ceremony, serving Miss Julie her tea first and ending with the colonel. There was also a tray of small sandwiches and one of delicate pastries, both served in a grand style.

They got on well, Julie and the colonel, and slowly Calero began to relax.

Time passed pleasantly as the shadows lengthened, and then the colonel turned serious.

"So, we come to the troublesome matter of the attempted fraudulent theft of your land, Miss Julie." He moved to his desk and picked up a heavy tooled-leather folder containing a long yellow legal pad, its pages filled with writing. "Ms. de Grut has provided me with many details. As you may have guessed, at my age I practice very little law these days; however, this gross injustice to two women who have given so much to their community causes me to feel rejuvenated!"

"Praise the Lord, brother," Calero said under his breath.

"You'll take the case then, Colonel?" Miss Julie asked, leaning forward.

"Oh, yes. I've already taken the case. We need only work out the contingency fee. My usual fee is one-third of the settlement. But, since I'm retired and my needs are simple…," he paused to wink at Calero, "when we win, I will be honored to accept twenty percent of the settlement. If we should lose, then honor demands that it cost you nothing, Miss Julie."

Julie looked at Calero and, seeing his nod of agreement, said, "I am honored to be represented by you, sir." She rose and took the colonel's hand.

"Fine! Let us seal our arrangement with some sherry. We can have it on the veranda while we watch the sun set on Sinnobar Hills."

After enjoying a glass of exquisite sherry and declining a gracious invitation to stay for dinner, Julie and Calero said good night to the colonel. Then their limousine slipped quietly down the hill and sped away, carrying in it two very satisfied and happy people.

11

A Brush with the Horns

As Domingo watched Calero drive away, he felt fear. Was it because he sensed Calero heard the music again? I'm worried, Domingo was thinking. Calero's step seems too light today. He thinks he is invincible, that no horns can get him. I think he believes if he were in the arena today, even if it were raining, the slippers that he wears would not get wet, and the bull would just lie down and die. Mustachio was not of this earth right now—and that was dangerous.

Driving south on the main highway out of Sinnobar Hills, Calero felt fully in control at the wheel of Nola's Cadillac Alante. He leveled the speed at fifty-five, punched cruise control, then settled easily into the luxury of the leather seat. The countryside sparkled in the afternoon sun; everything seemed to have crisp edges, vibrant color. He could almost feel the electricity in the air. There were other cars on the road, but Calero felt there was no one sharing his world but Nola.

It had been easy once he had made up his mind to win the lady. And this was not just any lady, this was Nola Rodriguez. Nola, with a scent that drove him wild and clothes that cried out to be slowly removed. This wasn't a familiar game he played with the women who came into his life—where he gambled and won. This was Nola, with playful dark eyes. Nola, who filled his mind with lust and made all the songs on the radio about love make sense. This was the woman whose very look and smell could make him begin to grow hard.

"What are you thinking, my big man?" Nola half-whispered it as her hand drifted over his hand where it rested on the gear shift. A shock of pleasure raced through him and his dark Spanish face grew hot and deepened in color. Eyes narrowed, he concentrated on the road ahead and said nothing. Flooded with heat, he would have only gasped with desire if he had opened his mouth.

"Nola got your tongue, Calero *mio?*" she asked playfully, looking like an innocent teenage tease as she slid against the passenger door. The clinging peach-colored silk dress she wore added softness to her dark hair and eyes but also drew his attention to her breasts so titillatingly displayed.

Realizing he'd been holding his breath, Calero tried to exhale slowly so she wouldn't notice what was building between his legs.

"It's a nice day for a drive, ma'am...nice car...nice lady...nice..."

"Cut the *toro mierda*, Calero," Nola interrupted him. "*'Senor Feliz'* there in your lap can't hide what's on his mind." She glanced at his crotch and moved her hand to his knee. As she slid closer to him, Calero wondered if wearing tight Levi's might have given him better body control.

"We have been attracted to each other since the first time I saw you in the coffee shop," Nola said.

Coming to the Los Banos turnoff then, the traffic occupied Calero's attention, and they drove on in silence. His mind, however, raced back to their accidental and innocent meeting after the hearing on the fate of his ranch. But it wasn't innocent—he knew even then that he would first cape her to his side and then into bed. Just like the others. But something had gone wrong. Nola had started to get inside his head and his heart during that first restaurant encounter—and now this!

He was losing control, falling in love, falling apart...and loving every minute of it. She had touched him that day, and he had been surprised when the magnetism between them generated a torrent of emotions that made his heart beat faster and his body leap to life in a new way. Leaving her that day he had felt like Manolete, the great bull fighter. He could do anything, he loved everyone; even more...he loved just being alive!

He brought the Alante to a halt in front of the Adobe Ranch Restaurant and Motel. It had recently reopened under new management, and for a while the regulars were going elsewhere. Good! More private that way. The place would be theirs for the evening, maybe all night if he got lucky.

Jumping out of the car, he hurried to open the door on Nola's side, bowing slightly as he extended his hand. She didn't get right out but swung her legs around and hesitated.

"Happy to be with me?" she asked, flashing a beautiful smile that showed the tip of her tongue.

"More than I know how to tell you," he said, and he let out a deep breath as he slowly pulled her out of the car. She came up against him, their lips and the tips of their tongues meeting.

They continued to stand there, holding each other. Nola's head slid to one side, and he buried his face eagerly in the long black hair that fell to her shoulders. As they pressed and rubbed slowly against each other, Calero didn't care how hard he got.

Suddenly, their mood was broken as Calero became alert to danger.

"Shit," he muttered.

"What is it?" Nola broke away from him, alarm in her voice.

"Inside...now!" he commanded, and pushed her toward the entrance. She hurried the few steps to the door of the restaurant and went inside without a word.

"Shit! No gun," he hissed, his right hand going to his left side. There were two men coming close now. Calero sensed the smell of ex-cons, looking for a car, a nice yellow car—Nola's car.

"What'd you say, bro?" the man closest to him asked as he sneered.

"I said I smell shit and it's not on the bottom of my shoe," Calero roared as he raised his right foot. Then he stepped quickly to the right as the man lunged, missing Calero's neck and catching a huge shoulder block square in the chest. Pivoting to the left, Calero smashed the other man full in the face with a bone-crunching right. That one went out and down. The other was struggling to get his wind back as he leaned against Nola's car.

"Damn, this is too easy," Calero said, and backed away, leaving the first attacker to rest and catch his breath. With twenty feet separating them, the attacker was emboldened again, but Calero stopped his advance by moving slowly forward and calling, *"Toro! Toro, aqui!"*

"What did you say, spic?" The man screamed it at him.

With a smile flickering across his lips, Calero baited him. "Come here, piece of shit."

Murder in his eyes, the man charged. Spinning away, Calero brought his left fist crashing into the back of the man's neck, felling him to the ground. "Down, out, and not moving," murmured Calero as he peered at the prone figure on the ground. Then, *"Ole!"* he shouted and strutted away, hearing in his mind the music played in the arena as a bull is dragged from the ring after a kill. He stopped and turned triumphantly, head in the air. Then he came back to the here and now.

The second man to go down, still sitting in the dust, was trying to stop a bad nosebleed.

"Hey!" Calero yelled. "Pick up this bullshit, load it in the back of your truck and drive north."

The appointed loader worked fast, never saying a word. Calero figured any man would have a hard time talking with a broken nose and a fractured jaw.

His job done, the bruised thug jumped into his truck and was ready to go when Calero hailed him. "Go north and don't stop until you get back where you belong. You know where you came from—or do you want me to tell you exactly where shit like you belongs?" Not waiting for an answer, he continued. "I've one more request and you'd better follow this one to the letter."

Staring at the man's nose, Calero knew fear was leaking out of it along with the blood. "Drive out of here, turn north, then wave and smile. Got it? Wave and smile! Your mother would like that, and it will keep me from…from…hand-cuffing you with bailing wire and turning you over to the sheriff…you escapee from San Quentin's shitpile!"

Calero's eyes narrowed. Was he right about the men? He wasn't sure, and calling the cops could only mean trouble for him, a long report—and no Nola today…

He saw the truck move away and then stop. The driver struggled to speak. "Thanks for letting us go," he called. "How did you know?…About San Quentin…?"

Calero shrugged and waved the truck away as he walked slowly back to Nola's car. "I didn't know, *pendejo*," he whispered to himself, "you just told me."

Turning on the ignition key, he pulled a car phone from the console, got the number for the anonymous witness program, and called it. Someone answered, and he spoke briefly. Then he went to join his Nola.

He pushed open the heavy door and waited for his eyes to adjust to the dim light. The place was just as he remembered it, but empty now except for the bartender at the large oak Spanish-style bar. He nodded, and then passed through to the dining room, where he found Nola sitting at a corner table and sipping what looked like a margarita. She smiled and threw him a kiss.

Very tired now, he sat down heavily. He pushed the melting margarita away with his good hand. The one that had dropped the attacker lay useless in his lap and it hurt badly. He wanted to hide it but didn't know how long he could.

"Please forgive the delay, Nola. I never like to keep a lady waiting."

Trying to hide her concern behind a mask of casual beauty, Nola leaned toward him and asked, "A margarita or champagne for the returning hero?"

"Champagne...and two ice buckets, please."

"What happened out there?" she asked, her alarm apparent.

"Oh, just a couple of lowlifers needing work. Jesus, I need the champagne. Waiter! *Mesero*, champagne, *ahora*. Your best, and two ice buckets. *Comprende?*" The waiter nodded and scurried to the bar where he spoke frantically to the bartender.

"Now then, Calero," Nola said, "let me see your hand...and tell me about that storm out there."

"Well, those two needed a lot."

"Calero!"

"Well...they needed a home...they needed an education...and they needed a job. So, I gave them all three. Can't we just leave it at that?"

The waiter arrived with the two ice buckets. *"Aqui, senor."*

"Put one on my right and one on the left," Calero directed, and then slowly raised his swollen hand and shoved it into the ice, wincing in pain as he did so.

"Jesus Christ!" Nola gasped. "What happened to your hand?"

"Oh, my hand? Waiter!"

"Si, senor?"

"Please cover my hand with that napkin...it's disturbing the lady."

Nola was impressed. "God, I like your style!"

Pleased, Calero nodded to the waiter. "You may pour the champagne, then bring us nachos and some very hot sauce."

"Inmediatamente!" The waiter bowed slightly in honor of one whom he felt deserved respect.

The rest of the evening was wonderful as Nola and Calero shared stories about their lives, talking until the restaurant closed. Calero was feeling increasing pain in his hand, however, and Nola finally told him, "Come on, I'm driving you home."

While Calero was paying the bill, Nola called the waiter over and asked, "How much for an ice-bucket...with fresh ice?" She handed him a hundred dollar bill. "Will this take care of it?"

"I'm sure that will be fine." The waiter was obviously impressed.

"Put the bucket in the yellow Alante parked outside...in the front seat on the passenger side. Got it?"

"Yes, ma'am. It'll be there, and I'll cover it with this nice white napkin." He hurried off to do her bidding.

Nola drove them home, and although she begged Calero to let her take him to the hospital, he absolutely refused. Nola thought his hand was broken; he knew it wasn't. By the time they reached the ranch, however, Calero had nearly passed out from the pain. Domingo, looking on disapprovingly as Calero kissed Nola good night, helped Calero into the house as Nola drove away.

Once in the house, Domingo pulled off Calero's boots, and Calero stretched out on his bed and closed his eyes. In his mind he kept seeing Nola swaying before him, and he wanted her.

Meanwhile, Domingo had left the bedroom, but soon returned with an ice-pack and a bottle of tequila. Examining Calero's hand, he sighed. "The hand will be fine…your heart, maybe no. When you fight the bull, use the cape, the sword…even a gun. But not your hands! *Mano a mano* one more time, Mustachio?"

Domingo sighed again before adding, "The woman is very beautiful…and very dangerous, I think. Do you believe you have found the one to marry and start a family?"

Calero smiled through his pain. "I'm not going to start the second half of my life until I'm fifty. Like you, Domingo, I am going to live to be a hundred."

"You think so, huh? Only a few men and a very few skilled bullfighters have a chance at a second life. Remember this, Mustachio. You go into the wrong arena and you will end up like your father. A matador must go slowly, from one bullring to the next, until finally he is ready for the *grande plaza de toros.* Your father tried to jump ahead too soon…and met the horns when he was only thirty. It was a woman like this one tonight who lured him into the wrong arena."

"Goddamn it, Domingo. Must you put everything in bullfight terms? This woman is just flesh and blood, like all the rest," he lied.

"Forgive me, but you are already a wise man? You are charging in the wrong arena, *toro.* This is not a woman for you. She will never stir the beans and feed the chickens. She will possess you, and blind you to the horns with her long black hair." Walking out of the room, he murmured, *"Buenas noches,* Mustachio."

"Buenas noches." Calero shook his head despairingly. Then, exhaustion and tequila dulling the pain in his hand, he drifted off into sleep, dreaming of Nola's hands, her body, being in her arms.

The next morning he woke from sluggish sleep to hear Olga yelling up the stairs. "Hey, we got a ranch to run, Calero. The phone is ringing off the hook again...and a couple of cops are here who want to say 'Howdy.'"

Calero groaned and, favoring his swollen hand, managed to dress. Once he was downstairs, the two officers told Calero the ex-cons he had run into the night before had been carrying a loaded shotgun in their truck. "They told us 'some spic in a yellow Cadillac' beat them up for no reason."

That caused Calero to comment that maybe the thugs should have used their shotgun on that "spic."

"Come on!" One of the officers laughed. "We know it was you, Calero. Every 911 operator and sheriff around here knows your voice."

"But, sir, I am a Spaniard known for my kindness to animals. They were animals, no?"

"Well, your animals are locked back up in San Quentin now. What happened to your hand?"

Calero grinned. "I was in a bullfight, *senors,* and unfortunately, I did not have my sword."

12

Triangle Sand and Gravel Company

"If Jerry 'Moonbeam' Brown can be governor of California, why not me?" Frank Rodriguez asked, leaning back in his expensive leather chair and surveying the men around him. His face was flushed with his feelings about his grandiose scheme. "I've got the wealth, the big yellow, and soon the mountain. We'll just buy whatever and whoever we need. We've got two years until the election. First we finish this business with the Davis sisters and put Calero under water. Then we concentrate on taking over the state."

Mayor Whisner spoke up. "I had to work my way up to become mayor—one damn committee after another. It was a slow process to the top. Had to pay a lot of dues and raise a lot of money." Whisner hated it when Rodriguez got too big for his chair.

"I'm not about to work my way up. Right? Just buy it! Right? Invest our own money, pay ourselves back after we win. Now, let's go over the plan again and see what progress we've made." Four men sat in Frank's office: Don Whisner, mayor; Jackson Busterud, banker; George Farley, real estate broker; and Frank, owner of the Triangle Sand and Gravel Company. Frank was considered "the kid" by the older men, but they were careful never to call him that to his face.

The men had gathered downtown in an old turn-of-the-century bank building. Frank liked the building because it looked like a fortress and was ostentatious. Nola didn't like it for those very reasons and knew Papa would have disapproved.

"Stay right on top of what you own and be with the folks that are making you rich," he had been fond of saying. "They appreciate it, and it shows we appreciate them." But after Papa died, Frank had purchased the old bank, kicked out the tenants, and had the building restored right down to the gold fittings in the bathrooms.

Against the wishes and strong objections of the man who was president of Triangle Sand and Gravel, Frank kept company gold in the old safe. Risky? Yes, but Frank liked risk and enjoyed entering the vault and seeing the gold behind the double security bars. In the 1930s, when the bank was in full operation, the old safe had been blown into the center of the street when some safe crackers had used too much dynamite.

Frank liked to tease Nola about keeping the gold in the old vault. Sure, Nola had warned him that it was a mistake to take over the old bank building and redo it in such a grand manner, and the ornate double-entry doors into his office and the palatial waiting room where his secretary sat was just too much for her.

The ornate grey building was Frank's command center. It even had what he called his "war room." He kept his dad's old office at the main plant but rarely went there. Too dusty and uncivilized. Too far away from his friends and the three older men now sitting in his office making powerful plans.

Frank's richly appointed office, overlooking everything down on the main floor, added to the feeling of his own importance. Those who came to see him had to walk up the sweeping stairs. He liked his plant managers having to parade up the stairs to his office, their feet soundless as they sank into the lush, thick carpeting.

Frank felt like a king. He was king now that Papa was gone. He was sitting on top of the mountain—the Triangle Sand and Gravel Company—and the mountain was made of gold and getting bigger every day. He would not allow his sister to stand in his way—no one would stand in his way, not even the old farts who, for now, were useful to him.

And how he loved going around both the president and vice-president of the company. They feared him because he could replace them at any time. Frank's father had put professional managers in place and rarely interfered, but Frank was everywhere, making notes, taking names, building an intelligence system.

The president of the Triangle Sand and Gravel Company was well aware that his days were numbered. The vice-president of the Land Company, a division of the main one, was a beautiful woman, the only powerful woman in the company, and she had Frank's number or she would have already been gone. She knew too many of his secrets, and an awful lot about the Calero Ranch, and other land holdings. And where the new gold deposits were.

The geologists and the shakers (those who reclaimed the gold at the bottom of the pits) worked under this capable woman. Frank needed her, and whenever he started to push her around, she would just stand firmly, put her hands on his desk and lean toward him. "That's not gonna happen, Frank," she would say, and then he would back down. The woman knew him as a coward without ethics, a rich businessman without a conscience, and she hoped he wasn't headed for disaster—for Nola's as well as the company's sake.

She would not have liked what she heard had she been in on the meeting of Frank and his co-conspirators. In response to Frank's question about progress that had been made, the banker, Jackson Busterud, spoke first. "We are on course on our end. Calero's loan won't be renewed this fall and we may be able to call in a large note that he used his stable as security on. Whisner here's got the county in line and they'll withhold the stable lease, so we got him by the balls there. Anything you got to add to that, Mayor?"

"Got four out of five county supervisors right here in this pocket," Mayor Whisner said, patting his breast pocket. "They want the lake expanded as much as we do, so they'll support the extension of the city limits to incorporate Rancho Calero. Once that's done, we condemn the place. We have the votes since the three of us here are on the city council."

"Farley," Frank said, "the ball's in your court on the real estate thing. How you doing with that old bag...the twin that's left?"

Frank had sneered when he said it, and George Farley winced at the "old bag" remark. He had always liked the twins; they had been like family at one time. But now that Frank owned him, he was in so deep he could see only two ways out—prison or a suitcase full of money. The latter appealed to him more.

For a moment, Farley flashed back to the early morning phone call he'd received and his confusion about Dial-A-Prayer. And then the gut-wrenching realization that something was about to go very wrong with his day. How wrong he hadn't known until he walked into his office and found Calero sitting there. He'd been sure he was going to die, either from a bullet or a heart attack. With those thoughts passing through his mind, he began to sweat as profusely as when Calero had confronted him. He felt he should report what had happened but feared Frank's reaction.

"Farley!"

"Huh?"

"Where the hell were you—you seem to have left the goddamn room," Frank yelled.

"Oh, yeah." Farley thought quickly, and shifting into his con man role, he decided to lie. Slipping behind his real estate broker shield, he lied convincingly. "Miss Julie's no problem," he said. "She never reads any of the documents I bring her—she just asks where to sign. The sister that died used to handle all their business matters. Miss Julie agreed to let me appraise the property for possible sale—that's the first step to set a low value. Then we'll buy it, just like we did that piece of theirs in Santa Clara. Miss Julie is so naive she'll sign. I'm seeing her this afternoon. Could get the job done today." Farley settled back in his chair, feeling relieved at having gotten past Frank for the time being. But the burning in his gut and perspiration under his arms told the real story. He was wet with fear and he could smell it.

"Another one of those old switcharoos, huh, George?" Frank smiled approvingly and the others snickered. "But we have to end this meeting soon," Frank went on, "our secret weapon, Nola, will be coming in to report. She's got Calero about tied up and ready for the TS&G brand. I don't want her to know we're in this together. Let's adjourn to the war room and you fellows can slip out after she arrives."

The four men traipsed down the stairs past Minerva, Frank's shapely secretary, and the other office staff. "Minerva, send Nola directly up to my office when she arrives. Tell her I'll be returning shortly."

They walked past the sealed vault. Its stainless steel glistened; the timed combination was shut. Few things made Frank's heart pound faster than running his hand over the shiny surface of the vault door.

No one but Frank had a key to the heavily reinforced door of the war room. When he inserted the key, it turned easily in the lock and the powerful dead bolt slid free. Frank turned the knob and the rather massive door swung open.

The men entered the room, stark in its contrast to the opulent outer surroundings. On the walls were a huge writing board, enlarged county and city maps, and an aerial photo of Rancho Calero lands. The room's windows were barred, the shades drawn; but the large board was uncovered, and on it were figures and a list of objectives boldly printed and numbered.

"Shit, Frank. Why isn't that stuff covered up?" Busterud snapped.

"Relax, Jackson. No one has access to this room but me. The room has an alarm system, and besides, if anyone saw the board, they wouldn't understand it."

Mayor Whisner added, "They sure would wonder why those names were up there next to the objectives."

They all hated this about Frank. Overconfident, he thought himself invincible. Busterud was worried and thought to himself that he wished Frank had a good dose of paranoia. Great leaders were paranoid, not just grandiose.

"Whisner's right about those names," the other two men chorused.

"We can't be too careful. There's too much money in it and too much risk," the mayor said, his mouth suddenly dry.

"Nola come in here, Frank? What about the cleaning lady?" Farley asked nervously.

"No on both counts…Well, the cleaning lady once in a while. She's a dumb Mexican who can't read or write her own language. I like them illiterate. That way all this information is secure." Frank frowned then. "What is this, the third degree? Just do your jobs and this general will do the rest," he said, and closed concealing doors over the plan on the board.

The intercom buzzed and Frank answered. "Thanks. Tell her I'll be right up."

The four trooped out, looking furtively up the stairs, but Nola was nowhere to be seen and the three older men made their escape. After securing the war room, Frank bounded up the stairs to his office and hugged his sister waiting there. He loved her; she was all he had. And she'd do anything for him, just like his mother had. He liked that.

They sat together on the office couch. He reached for her hand, but she looked away. "Hey! Sis."

"Frank, I don't know where to start," Nola said with a deep sigh. "I think I'm falling in love."

"Well, that's wonderful, Sis...who is it?"

"Oh, Frank...it's Calero I'm in love with!"

He shot up from the couch, his mind whirling. "You can't do this to me, Nola!" he snapped at her.

"I had no intention of falling in love with that strange man. When you suggested I put the moves on him, I just didn't think I could do it. How could I ever be attracted to a man I thought would smell like a barn? But I found out he's a lot like Papa was. He's built like him, and he's rough and yet gentle at the same time. And he's always immaculate...and Calero is very bright, Frank. You'd like him."

"Shut up!" Cold as stone now, Frank stood glaring down at her. "Remember what your job is! You're not supposed to love this stupid Spaniard, you're to get him off that land!"

"Maybe he'd give up the land for me. Move into the city, work for the company, start a family. Oh, Frank, I do think I love him."

"Never!" Frank shouted at her. There's no way you'll ever bring that lowlife Spaniard from a two-bit bullfighting family into ours. Never! What would the big jerk do for the company? Drive a cement truck?"

"Damn it, Frank. How can you say such things?" Angry now, too, Nola jumped to her feet, her hands on her hips. "His grandfather was a famous bullfighter and so was his father. They were proud, rich, famous people long before our family was much of anything."

"The truth is, Nola, that his father was an idiot who died in the Tijuana ring because he wasn't any good. No good—just like Calero. A nothing to be gotten out of the way. Before he came to Rancho Calero ten years ago, Calero was living under the power lines, kissing Gorman the goat man's ass to keep a pathetic stable going. Gorman kicked him out because Calero couldn't pay the rent.

"He was broke then and he's about to be broke again. He just wants your money and status. He'll never be anything more than a dude ranch operator—a failure. I'm going to drive him back to where he came from. Back under the power lines with Gorman the German and his goats and filthy stables. Get your act together, Nola. We've got a business to run and an empire to build."

Obviously distressed, Nola pleaded with him, "But I'm not getting any younger, Frank. I want a family. I'm tired of playing around. My biological clock is ticking. There's more to life than money and power, and for me I think it's love…family…Calero…"

"Stop it!" Frank raged, grabbing and shaking her. "We made a pact, you and me, when Dad died. We decided to build an empire—and no ignorant Spaniard with a bent sword in his pants is going to change that." Sneering now, he asked his sister, "Tell me, Nola, do you ever feel like you're sleeping with Papa when you are with Calero?"

"You're disgusting, Frank." Nola was on the verge of tears.

"Maybe I am, but I have to reach you, honey." Cunning and manipulative, Frank went on talking. "God, you've got to come to your senses. Damn it—Go see Doc Kansky, he'll help you through this. You've fallen in love before…

remember your sky diving instructor? These things come and go. All affairs of the heart come and go."

"I don't know, Frank. I just don't know. Maybe you're right."

"Of course I'm right, honey. Have fun, damn it. Fall in love, damn it. But don't bring bad blood into our family. We're Mexican and proud of it, with a little Cherokee thrown in. That should help us never forget that a tribe has to stick together. Remember what Papa said? 'You two must pledge to work as one if anything happens to me. Promise?' Remember that, Nola?"

At her nod, he went on, turning into the soft helpless little boy she couldn't keep from mothering. "We promised, Nola. We promised," Frank said.

"I know, Frank, but I just can't seem to stop caring about him. He's so vulnerable, so sad sometimes. I think it might kill him if I reject him."

Frank turned toward the window so his sister wouldn't see the cruel smile that curled the corners of his mouth. "I'm lonely, too, Nola, and I need you to help me…just like when we were kids. I can't handle this alone. First Mama leaves, then Papa, and now maybe you. I'm the one who just might die." Frank blinked tears into his eyes by looking into the sunlight streaming in through a crack in the blinds—a trick he'd learned as a child. It had always worked with Nola but never with his father. Tears in place, he turned toward Nola.

"Oh, Frank, don't cry," she said, and going to him, she put her arms around him.

Poor Nola, Frank thought, she was so easy. Even as a kid she would do his homework, cover for him when he lied, and always see that he got the best horse to ride. She was too much like Papa with his giving nature. "Walk in the ditch," he would say. "Don't do the obvious—but always be honest, keep your word, and work for the good of the people. Remember, Frank, true happiness comes from helping others."

That's not my philosophy, Frank thought. My happiness comes from winning. Winning at any cost. And people? All of them are expendable—fair game.

For a moment, he stood quietly, hugging his sister. Then she kissed his cheek and moved toward the door. "I have to go, Frank. I'll do what you ask, but it won't be easy."

"Nola, I love you," he called after her.

She stopped, but didn't answer him before she rushed down the stairs and out of the building.

Frank's face hardened. He wiped away the deceptive tears and without another thought about Nola tackled the stack of paperwork on his desk. He felt good—in control. A couple of hours passed before he heard the commotion downstairs.

"He's in his office," he heard Minerva's voice announce. "I'll let him know you're here."

"Crap," Farley said, and then spun around and took to the stairs, bursting through Frank's office doors just as Minerva reached Frank on the intercom.

"We are in fucking-A big trouble, Frank!" Farley spit out the words as he stood facing the paper-strewn desk.

"Calm down, Farley...and try to stop sweating. What's this all about?"

Pacing back and forth, Farley unloaded his bombshell. "I went to see Miss Julie today, Frank, like I said I would, and she was very cool toward me. Not her usual offer of tea or anything. Her bags were stacked in the front hallway and she told me she was going on a long cruise. I gave her the papers to sign, but, instead of signing them, she put them in her desk and locked it. Then she said that she and Mr. Calero would review them in good time. And that was it. I was ushered to the door. Calero's going to see through it, Frank. In fact, I'm afraid he already has."

"You dumb son of a bitch! I told you to make the switch on the hill first. But, no, you had to go after the piece in Santa Clara—wanted the big commission."

Farley interrupted him. "More bad news, Frank. Calero's on to the Santa Clara deal—he put the squeeze on me this morning. I didn't want to worry you earlier, but he put a hard squeeze on me...came to my office...I thought he was going to kill me. He was sitting behind the door when I came into my office and he scared the shit out of me. That arrogant, two-bit, never-was bullfighter said he was prayin' for me that I'd kill the escrow deal. I tell you, he has it all figured out. We're in real trouble, Frank...real trouble." Farley appeared close to tears.

I should kill the bastard right now and put him out of his sweating, bumbling misery, Frank thought. But it couldn't be here, not yet. As much as he was ready to do the deed at that very moment, he knew it couldn't be here in the office. His crafty mind began to formulate a plan. He became cool and collected, a general without feelings. "It looks like we're left with only one alternative, Farley. We take Calero out—permanently—just like his barking dog."

"Frank! I don't want any part of that kind of thing and that's..."

"Shut up and leave it to me, Farley. Relax. Things may have just gotten real simple. Come on, I'll see you out." Frank, calm and cold, led the shaken real estate broker to the front door.

"Frank, what should I do?" Farley's voice contained none of the bravado he usually displayed.

"Go home and take a shower, Farley; you stink like a sweaty saddle."

Frank turned away as Farley left and went quickly to the board in his war room. Opening the doors that covered the plan, he drew an X through Calero's name. Picking up the phone, he dialed slowly, and when it was answered, he said simply, "Got a job for you. It's time to take him out... Yes, an accident would be best."

13

A Sword Meant for Calero

As he drove along the road, Calero's thoughts were all on Nola. "Oh, Nola, I love you so," he murmured. "Can't think of anything but you…Nothing seems to matter but to be near you, hold you…touch you…make love to you." As his mind wandered, so did the truck. A car horn blared and startled him, and he saw the driver rage at him as he passed.

Smiling, Calero waved, then slipped in a cassette of Lou Rawls' "Let Me Be Good to You." He moved in rhythm with the music, thoughts of Nola filling his mind. It's Sunday afternoon…what are you doing, baby?

They had gotten serious so fast it didn't make sense. They didn't care, they were in love, trusting each other completely, nothing held back. Pulling out all the stops—risking everything.

"God, it feels good!" he yelled aloud. Then he was back to his thoughts. It seemed such a long time ago that they had walked up Sinnobar Hill and stood looking out over the still water of the lake—talking and sharing what they felt they needed out of life. I felt I needed freedom, Calero thought, and she needed intimacy. By that I thought she meant sex—she didn't.

"I need the intimacy that only comes from being complete with a man, secure, warm by the fire, with a baby in my arms. I want a new life, in a new home in town, where the kids can go to good schools," she had told him.

He had wanted none of that before, but now he knew he would do anything for her. He was ready! No more arguments about it—marriage, live in town, kids, work for the company—whatever Nola wanted. Just so he didn't lose her.

It felt good to put her first in everything, letting go, giving himself over to her—living for the intimacy, the closeness and love. Whenever she pulled away in the slightest, he was seized with panic, and would be in a living hell until she beckoned him, touched him, reassured him she would always love him. Then ecstasy, passion and unbelievable sex.

To hell with Domingo and his outdated ideas about women. To hell with the mystical nonsense whispered into his head by the so-called Black Widow, an uneducated stage-coach teamster. Nola was the perfect woman and he wanted her more than life itself. He heard himself saying it, "Give me Nola for life, or my life is over."

Elation filled him. He felt more complete than ever before, as if he were floating on top of the universe. A picture of Nola and himself, naked and entwined, sailing through clouds, flashed before his eyes. Then the jarring of the highway divider bumps brought him back to reality, and he swerved away from a car on his right. "Shit! Watch where you're going, Calero," he chided himself.

But his thoughts were immediately back on Nola. And how Domingo always twisted things. Like when Nola got him to shave off his mustache. It tickled her when they made love, that was all, but Domingo had to make a big deal of it. "When a man changes his looks for a woman, he's either a little boy or the lover of an evil one who will take away his *cojones*, his strength, his will to resist. And, Mustachio, you are no little boy."

It had been pretty good symbolism, Calero thought. Domingo would have made a good shrink.

"I know you shaved off that silly mustache because you love me," Nola had said, tugging at her clothes and beckoning with her eyes for help. Then the lovemaking had swept them away.

Why did Domingo's primitive musings have such an effect on him, he wondered. He was through sharing with Domingo. No matter what he told him, the old man twisted it and gave it back to him in a way he least wanted to hear.

Like the chocolate milk story. Domingo couldn't get off it. "Remember when you were a little boy and wanted chocolate milk? When your mother said no and pushed you out of the house, you went crying to grandmother's house. She gave you chocolate milk and a hug. When you choose the woman you want to be with for the rest of your days, my friend, choose one who will give you chocolate milk and hugs. Test this Nola woman."

One evening, Calero had done just that. He and Nola were alone in his old house. After a wonderful day together, they were sitting contentedly by the fire, and it was then that he tested her. Stretching, he asked, "Fix me some chocolate milk, Nola? There's some in the cupboard—I love chocolate milk."

"God, Calero, don't be a baby. If you want chocolate milk, fix it yourself. That's not a man's drink, it's a little boy's drink. I'm going up to bed."

Stunned and hurt, Calero had moved slowly to follow her. In the hallway, he passed family pictures—first, one of his mother, then his grandmother. He turned back to the kitchen then, going to the refrigerator and pouring himself a glass of milk. He took a long sip. Then he reached for the chocolate.

He had lain awake that night, feeling alone. Nola slept motionlessly. He didn't touch her at all, but in the morning she had come to him. Everything was forgotten in the morning, eclipsed by the lovemaking. The new chocolate milk in his life was the deep satisfaction that only Nola could provide. Ha! What did Domingo know.

As he continued driving along the busy highway, Calero brought his thoughts back to the present. Things were going so well, he didn't know why he was bothering to keep the appointment he had in Santa Clara today. I could be with Nola right now, he thought. Then he recalled the strange dream he'd had the night before. Same old bullring, but this time no bull. The arena filled with people, music and cheers, but when the shoot opened, no charging bull.

I am there in the arena. I am inching forward calling, "Toro! Toro, aqui." I stamp my foot and look off to one side as the audience begins to whistle and jeer. I sweat with embarrassment. Then I see her—a blonde woman beckoning to me from the stands. Her voice carries above the noise and reaches my ear. "Run away with me," she calls.

Noise from the shoot draws me to its dim depth. Moving closer and peering in, I see a dark tombstone. It falls toward me and I jump back. Now the sound of pounding hoofs comes from behind, and I turn in time to see a wedge, a perfect triangle of men, of male flamenco dancers bearing down on me. Frantically, I spin and execute the Pacheco Pass but am caught by the lead dancer and tossed high into the air. Wounded and bleeding, I land atop the dancers and they sweep me into the shoot.

Calero shook himself free of the nightmarelike reverie and turned his attention to the road. That dream had scared the hell out of him. As he exited the freeway, a flat-bed truck, loaded with steel bars, accelerated past and swerved in front of him.

"What the...?" The bed of the truck began to rise as both vehicles moved along the off-ramp. Nowhere to get away— cement barriers on both sides—a death trap. In a split second, Calero checked the rearview mirror. All clear. He slammed on the brakes and riveted his attention on the steel bars hitting the pavement, sending sparks in every direction, then pin-wheeling toward him like propellers flying loose from an airplane.

As he spotted the most dangerous piece coming directly at him, everything seemed to go into slow motion. Totally controlled, he waited in the skidding, decelerating truck for the rusty instrument of death headed toward his windshield. It had flown off with all the rest of the bars, but this particular sword was meant for him. The steel hit the truck's hood, bounced, and flew straight through the windshield. Never taking his eyes off the bar, at the last second he turned in his seat like a matador caping a bull, and the steel passed through the open back window and thundered into the truck bed. As the truck skidded to a halt, other steel bars crashed into it.

Calero's first thought was of his dog Spooky, who always rode in the back, but of course he was not there this time. Then he watched as the truck ahead of him braked and almost stopped. Then it sped away.

"Your ass is mine, you son of a bitch," Calero said coldly, and bouncing over scattered steel bars, drove after the truck in angry pursuit. His own truck was running badly, steam pouring out of a hole in the hood. "Don't die yet, baby," he prayed, pushing the accelerator to the floor, "don't die yet."

The first truck didn't have the power of Calero's, however, and Calero was determined to affect a capture. Drawing his rifle from its scabbard in the door, he laid the weapon on the seat beside him. As he pulled alongside the fleeing enemy, he motioned the dark, sweating driver to stop, but the driver speeded up. Calero raised the rifle then, showing it, and at that the truck driver applied the brakes.

Calero cut in front of him and the two vehicles skidded off onto the dusty shoulder. As steam enveloped his truck and the engine clattered loudly, Calero calmly used his cellular phone to call for a cab. "Yes, right away…De la Cruz exit."

Cautiously then, he moved out of the truck on the passenger side and, tucking the rifle under his left arm, moved through the cloud of steam and dust. Jerking open the passenger door of the other truck, he stood back. The dark heavyset driver was staring straight ahead, his hands gripping the steering wheel tightly.

"*Comprende Ingles, muerto hombre?*"

"*Pequeno,*" the sweating man answered.

"Get down out of the truck on this side, and as you pass that glove compartment, bring only the registration. One false move, and you'll have to use your other hand to play with yourself. *Comprende?* Then we'll have a little talk about the way you unloaded that steel back there. I didn't like your method, *senor. Como se llama?*"

"Arturo Palacios," the man answered through trembling lips. Moving slowly, he appeared beaten and exhausted. Carrying out Calero's orders in a daze, he stepped down. Calero slammed the truck door, spun the man around and, pushing him against the truck, kicked the man's feet apart. "*Manos alto!*" Then he rested the barrel of the Winchester between the man's legs. "Say *adios* to your *huevos, muerto hombre.*"

"*Dios*, forgive me. I am sorry." The man's chest heaved with grief and he began to plead in broken English. "Spare my family…I give you my life. I have eight children…they are hungry. *Muchos problemas.*" Then, noticing Calero's ear out of the corner of his eye, "But you are bleeding, *senor.*" He stared at Calero's torn jacket and the blood dripping down on Calero's hand.

"No, it is you who are bleeding—from the inside out. You are a desperate man who could lose everything…and shed your family's blood as well, Arturo Palacios."

The frightened man shook his head. "I couldn't kill you back there. That's why I swerved the truck. The steel was supposed to miss you…it was my decision. They ordered me to kill you. Now they will kill me and then kill you later."

"They?" Calero questioned.

"I'm not supposed to know—but I do know. They think I am stupid and speak no English so they talk too much and reveal much. We all know and talk about it among ourselves at the *bracero* camp. The Triangle people are behind it," he said, and handed the truck registration back over his shoulder.

Calero glanced at it, then lowered the gun and ordered the man to sit back in the truck. He walked back to his own truck, scabbarded the rifle, and locked the doors. Then he returned to the seated man.

"Listen to me. That piece of steel in the back of my truck? I want you to leave it there. It's mine now. Clean up that mess back there on the road, then go home. Talk to no one. Be ready to leave the *bracero* camp tonight—you and your entire family. I will come for you. You work for me now."

As the man nodded eagerly, the taxi Calero had ordered arrived and Calero jumped in. "Santa Clara Mission," he said without a backward look, "and hurry."

14

A Raging Bull

Three hours later, after picking up his patched-up truck, Calero drove cautiously down the lane to the *bracero* camp. The long, rusty piece of steel that had nearly impaled him rattled in the back of the truck, and a large box of groceries on the seat beside him shifted as he swerved back and forth to miss the ruts. Lights flickering dimly through the trees softened the cruel edges of the migrant camp and dusk hid the sad eyes in children's faces.

Calero stopped at the first shack and asked in Spanish where he could find Arturo Palacios. No answer. He drove on, passing suspicious people standing in crooked doorways. Children playing in the dirt stared at the white pickup that was once again steaming from its injury.

A teenage Mexican boy suddenly appeared and beckoned to Calero to follow him through a narrow break between the shacks. Calero followed in the pickup, depressed by what he was seeing and feeling resigned. Just as these poor people's fate was sealed, so was his. It was over for him. They struggled to eat; he had struggled for love. Both humiliating games in the end.

He followed the boy's path into deepening shadows, knowing the risks and not caring. No matter what happened, he wouldn't defend himself. Let it end here. As he drove slowly on, his black mood gathered volume.

A large shack appeared ahead, but unlike the others, this one was neat—different. There was Arturo Palacios, clean clothes and all, standing proud in the center of his family. Round and shy, his pleasantly attractive *esposa*, a baby in her arms, smoothed the hair of the child who had buried her face in her mother's long cotton skirt. So many children, Calero thought—enough children to fill a one-room schoolhouse. The teenage boy, obviously the eldest, took a protective stance next to his father. *Senor* Arturo Palacios and his family were ready to meet and pledge their loyalty to their new *patron.*

Arturo rushed forward and bowed clumsily as Calero got out of the truck. The gesture startled Calero out of his depression. The blackness lifted as the joy that comes from helping others in need flooded through him. He felt waves of love for these children he didn't even know.

Arturo took Calero's hand and pulled him toward the center of the family. "This is *Don* Calero, our honored *patron.* He has saved my life and we owe him everything! Everything, my family! Our hands, our good work, our loyalty, and *su padre's existancia. Ninos, decie bienvenido, patron, bienvenido!*

The children said their welcome over and over again— Spanish mixed with English. Embarrassed, Calero cursed himself for hating life when he was surrounded by so many hopeful hearts. Gifts, he would give them gifts. Pulling away, he went to the truck and reached for the box of groceries.

"Help *Don* Calero, Miguel," Arturo commanded, pushing his son forward, and the sullen boy took the box.

"Thank you, thank you," chorused the littlest ones pulling on the edge of the large box to see and to smell.

"This is Maria, our littlest one, and this is..."Arturo proudly introduced each member of the family.

Calero didn't know what to say. He heard himself mumble, "You said you were hungry, so I brought a little food..."

"*Mil gracias, me nina necesita leche. Nada por tres dias,*" Arturo's wife explained as she grabbed the carton of milk and handed it to the oldest daughter, who fled with it into the house. Calero was thrilled at this reception of his gift, forgetting himself, his problems.

Then, quite suddenly, with no warning, the thought of Nola slashed through his mind. It was like a sharp sword hitting bone with a jarring crack. In his tortured mind he was in the arena again, saw the sword hit bone in the neck of a massive bull, then spring back into the air and narrowly miss the matador's stunned face.

"Oh, God, I have to see her!" He was unaware he had spoken aloud.

"What is it, *senor?* Are you all right? Can I get you something to drink?" It was Arturo asking him, a frightened look on his face.

"What?" Calero saw they were all staring at him, frozen as if in a picture where no one had expected to be photographed. How long had he stood there, imagining that scene with the bull?

The older daughter returned then with the baby's bottle filled with milk, and all eyes shifted to the whimpering hungry child.

"I must go, I have unfinished business in town. I must go." Calero spoke quickly, relieved the baby was now the center of attention. Going to his truck, he jerked open the door and called, "Domingo will come for you in the early morning. Be ready! You work for me now."

He was unprepared for Arturo's answer. "But I will not be here tomorrow," Arturo told him, heaviness in his voice. "I will be *muerto*...dead."

"What?!" Calero snapped the word out.

"The camp, it is sad tonight, and my son, he is tense because he knows. All the *braceros* know. Tonight, someone will come for me. Everyone knows that death will come."

The rage that swept over Calero was like a bull's reaction to the taunting toss of a *muleta*. *"Toro mierda,* you say!" And he spit.

"Si. Es verdad. I go with you or I die...and my family eats their last meal, for which Mary Mother of God blesses you."

Calero swore again. All life seemed a "hating thing." He would go, go kick that wicked bitch in the ass, say *adios*. Then he would cash in his chips because life sucked and...

He realized Arturo was still talking. "...I may deserve to die but my family does not deserve to starve. Help me, *Don* Calero, help my babies."

"Quiet!" Calero screamed it, slamming his head into the window of his truck as angry tears streamed down his cheeks.

Arturo walked back to his family and put his arm around his wife. His face registered the resignation of his long-suffering ancestors. He had done everything he could do.

Damn, damn, damn! Turning the key in the ignition, Calero snatched the truck phone out of its cradle and one by one smashed a rigid finger into the illuminated numbers.

"Domingo! Hurry over here...to the *bracero* camp. I need your help now. It's Arturo...I'm trying to help someone...many children..." Moments passed as the family stared. "Please help me, Domingo. We have to get Arturo Palacios and his family out of this hellhole camp and give them a chance. They're good human beings and they won't give up!" Maybe I will, but they won't, he thought.

Domingo broke in on Calero's pleas. "Listen to me! I know your anger and despair. I warned you of that woman. The blackness cannot kill you as long as you can stand, as long as you have the courage to cape the evil one, one more time. Roll away from the horns, push yourself up from the sand. Do it for me, Mustachio. Please do it for me."

Mustachio

"Okay, okay, it's not that serious," Calero lied. "It's just that this Mexican family is being abused and I can't stand it. I want you to come get the family—don't bitch—it's a big family. Put them in the empty ranger station house for now. I don't give a damn if it is federal property—just bust the locks off the door and settle them in. And they'll need protection." There was a pause while he listened to Domingo. "I know you won't like this, but they may need plenty of armed protection. Now listen...grab four Winchesters and four cautious men who are willing to shoot if they have to. Arm them and come to the *bracero* camp now. Bring the big truck to carry the family and their things and two backup vehicles to ride shotgun, and get here fast. There's something else I have to attend to."

"Thirty minutes," said Domingo and hung up.

Calero turned to Arturo and his frightened family. "Pack up! You're moving out of here in thirty minutes...all of you. I'm heading out to the entrance. Domingo will be here with armed men and you will all be safe." Then he revved up the truck and headed for the camp's entrance.

He hoped the enemy would show up. He wanted to hurt someone. He was ready to kill.

Speeding down the rutted road, he ignored the treacherous potholes. Every slam of the tires was a punch square in the face of someone he hated—Frank and his evil arrogant kind...and Nola, especially Nola. Bam! He willed the tires to blow to pieces.

Smashing on the brakes, he locked them and skidded across the lane, leaving only enough room for one vehicle to pass. Ripping off his hat, he propped it on the seatback so it would look like a man slumped in his seat. Pulling his Winchester from its scabbard, he slipped out of the truck and into the darkness. There he waited.

"I will you to come…you Triangle Sand and Gravel people are sick criminals," he whispered into the darkness.

Cars and time passed, then he saw them coming. They traveled fast, their lights carving a wedge ahead of them. Calero cocked his gun, and his brain focused with that singleness of purpose of the hunter with a beast in his rifle sight. Wait. Wait.

The first vehicle skidded to a stop, followed by two more. Light illuminated the white pickup and Calero saw Domingo jump from the lead truck and jerk open the door of the stalled truck. The decoy hat slid down to the seat.

"Oh…!" Domingo expelled air and then, with relief, sucked in more. "Good trick, Calero!" He tossed that off, then ran back to his truck, and signalling for the other trucks to follow, he sped down the lane.

Smiling, Calero stepped out of the shadows and got into his own truck. Behind him he could see tail lights darting up and down the rutted road into the *bracero* camp, and knew that Arturo and his family would now be safe.

Now he would drive toward Sinnobar Hills to find Nola— the evil one. He had but one thought in his mind. He had trouble putting it into words, but he knew how it would all end. Yes, he knew, goddamn it! He would tell her how her deceitful plotting, her careless handling of his love, had hurt and injured him to the point his life no longer had meaning. Then he would end the life of Joe Calero. A sick animal had to be put down. That's it—put down, removed. But, God, once he had loved her so.

As he drove faster and faster through the night, the curves in the road seemed smooth and fluid, even inviting. The powerful white Chevy with its now red-lined steaming engine had never screamed so quietly. Calero wondered if he pulled back on the wheel, would the Chevy fly?

Easy curves now. Where before many of them had whispered "caution," they now seemed to be saying to him, "Hello, would you like to die around the next bend? You could die here, *pendejo* spic, obscure Spaniard, clumsy overgrown Mexican, Tijuana trash without a father." Calero realized he was shouting the words out loud. Oddly enough, it felt good; he didn't care what anyone might say of him.

Damn you, Dad...critical dead padre, tormentor of the only son you ever had. A good son, a twelve-year-old big son. A clumsy son, but one who prayed that you would live and not die on the horns. A loyal son who only wanted a kiss before you died. Maybe all I wanted was a kiss, shithead father who took the horns and never came home. I loved you so, Papa, and now I don't care at all. Bye-bye, Papa.

Was that the answer? To no longer care? After all these years of wanting his father's approval, squinting his eyes, hoping to see a spark of approval—just don't care? And all those months of loving and giving to that cold rejecting beautiful bitch Nola, hoping for approval at the end of the suffering—just don't care?

So, if his love for his dead father and the scheming assassin Nola was to be denied—then he just wouldn't care! Maybe all the evil bumps of life would flatten out if he just didn't care. Then he was screaming into the shattered windshield, "Damn you, Nola, you bitch!"

More speed now. The Chevy seemed to float toward some destiny at a speed no mortal could handle. It was someone else at the wheel, staying the course, perhaps curious as to how Calero would handle the rest of his life. But as the truck approached the entrance to Black Hawk Villa Condominiums—Nola's home away from home—Calero took control.

The condo was where they had made love many times. As the guard station loomed ahead, the guard moved to intercept Calero. He knew he should check in, but he roared past the guard, looking straight ahead. He had only one thought now—catch her in the arms of one of her many boyfriends. Kill two birds with one hollow point fired at close range. That's the ticket. Get it over with while your guts are still filled with ice-water.

"Oh-oh," the guard said, dropping his clipboard and grabbing the phone as the white truck hit the speed bumps without slowing down. "Nice bounce, Mr. Calero," the guard said out loud as he recognized Miss Rodriguez's frequent guest.

He heard Nola answer the phone. "Good evening, Miss Nola, this is Charlie at the gate. Sorry to bother you, but your friend, Mr. Calero, just roared through the front entrance...hit the speed bumps...didn't look right or left...strange. Always real polite in the past so this seems kinda unusual. Want me to send around a patrol car?"

Nola received the call with mild concern. "No, Charlie, you sweet protective thing. I just am so pleased with how you look after me. None of the rest of the guards seem as concerned as you do, and I just adore you for it. When you're on duty I'm really safe, aren't I?"

"Yes, ma'am. I...um..." Charlie's lips went numb. He was about to renew his old habit of stuttering, but the woman he secretly admired and lusted after, who thrilled him and made his day, saved him by interrupting.

"Charlie, Charlie, you dear man. Mr. Calero is at the door now. I don't think he'll cause any trouble, but then again he could. Be a sweetheart and don't leave your office. If I hit the panic button, you call 911, grab your shotgun and come running. Okay?"

"Yes, ma'am, I sure will!" Charlie pledged it as Nola hung up.

Calero was now out of the truck and up the steps. Beautiful place...only the rich could live here. Ring the bell. Try the door. Wait. Nothing. Not a sound.

"You can't hide, you fornicating bitch," Calero screamed into the carved front door, surprised by the angry sound of his voice. "The raging bull from Spain is here, killer bitch."

Drawing back, he looked at the impenetrable door, a barrier made to keep out man or beast. But a door he knew could not stop an enraged lover. He charged headlong at it and the impact on his shoulder dazed him, but the door, that impenetrable barrier, fell away like *papier-mâché*.

Calero didn't hear the wood scream as the deeply embedded screws resisted, weakened, then ripped free and flew toward the woman standing calmly by the fireplace. The heavy carved oak door smashed into the wall, its brass handle piercing the wall like a bull's horn and sticking fast. From somewhere there was a groan of human-sounding protest, then a black quiet filled the room.

15

Defeat

From the top of the hill, Calero looked back over his shoulder toward the ranch house and saw that it was dark and quiet now.

It had been cloudy all day and the night was strangely hot and humid. Heat lightning kept flashing across the sky. Calero felt more peaceful than he ever had before. He had made a decision. There was nothing left to do. He had lost Nola, he had lost faithful Spooky with the people-bark, and he had lost the final bullfight in his mind. It seemed nothing was left to live for.

He reached toward his left side, a gesture he had made so many times before, and now it would be for the last time. Standing with his feet planted firmly, he grasped the butt of the pistol and slowly drew it from its holster. Twisting the weapon upside down, he slowly placed it against his forehead. The barrel slid down his sweating face until it struck his teeth. Then the barrel entered his mouth, coming to rest cold and ready against the roof of his mouth. He pulled the hammer back and it clicked into place. The meaty part of his finger rested firmly on the trigger. He felt calm and at peace—he could let it all go.

Then the earth seemed to explode as a huge bolt of lightning lit up the night sky. Calero was so startled he jerked the pistol from his mouth, instinctively grabbing the hammer with his thumb and stopping its split-second movement toward the bullet. Still holding the hammer, he looked up, and another thunderous explosion followed a second brilliant strike of lightning that ripped open the sky. He felt a drop of rain on his face...another. Heavy rain beat against him, pounding the ground and drenching him. The long-awaited storm seemed to signal that the six-year drought the area had suffered was ending.

Calero slumped to the ground onto his knees and let the rain beat hard against his face and sweating body. As he continued to kneel, defeated, his head was filled with sounds of the boos and jeers of the bullring.

At last, with the pistol dangling from his right hand, his thumb off the hammer now, he rose and slowly began to trudge down the hill toward the house, leaving his fine white hat lying behind in the mud. Calero was a beaten man as he stumbled down the hill, his hair plastered against his face. Water was dripping off his shoulders and the barrel of his gun.

He pushed open the ranch gate, not caring whether he closed it or not, and moved toward the house. Calero noticed that a light was on in Domingo's *casita*, but he didn't want Domingo to see him. He moved on toward the barn, pushed open the door and walked to where a red exit bulb burned at the far end.

Domingo, who had heard the thunder and lightning and knew the horses would be frightened, had put on his yellow slicker and left his house just in time to see Calero pushing open the barn door.

Entering the barn, Domingo saw Calero at the far door-way, without his hat, a pistol dangling from his hand. The red glow of the exit light dimly illuminated the water streaming down Calero's body, making the water look like blood—blood dripping from a huge, dying bull.

Domingo's heart pounded and made a sickening descent into the pit of his stomach. *"Dios mio,"* he cried aloud, believing Calero had shot himself and was bleeding his life away. Running to Calero, he held him and begged, "Oh, my son, what have you done?"

Calero's answer was barely audible. "I'm all right. Just leave me alone."

Domingo jerked back and realized what he saw was water—not blood. "Leave you alone? *Dios!* Give me that gun and I'll kill you myself. Come to my *casita, pendejo.*"

Domingo pulled the pistol from Calero's hand, carefully setting the hammer back in place. With his arm around Calero's waist, he guided the big man, cursing in Spanish all the way to the *casita.* Domingo, no longer afraid, and filled with relief, was grateful that he had been given one more chance to save the grandson of his beloved friend, *Grande Padre Mustachio.*

Pushing Calero gently into a chair, Domingo lit a candle and extinguished the overhead light. He grasped a crucifix, pressed it into Calero's hand, and recited the prayer that is always recited over the injured bullfighter. Then he added, "Now, listen to me, son of a bitch. Now, I am going to tell you everything—everything about your grandfather, your father, and the evil one who is back among us."

16
The Fiesta of Love
Must Be Cancelled

Moving about his small kitchen, Domingo jerked open the cabinet and said, "But first, we need strong drink. Tequila to warm our guts and our hearts. Tequila to dull the pain and loosen our tongues. And here is *limon*—to make our mouths ready for what we are to say. And salt? We need salt to remind us of our tears."

He filled two small water glasses and set them on the table in front of Calero. Mumbling, Domingo returned to the kitchen, slammed two limes down on the counter and began to cut furiously.

"Drink, you son of a bitch. Try to kill yourself without telling me? Like father, like son. I could kill you myself with my bare hands."

Calero, frowning at Domingo who was still chopping away at the limes, called out, "What are you saying? I can't hear you, Domingo." Then he gulped half the searing liquid from his glass.

Whispering now as his tears flowed, Domingo spoke to the air. "I hate you, *Pequeno Mustachio,* for leaving me to raise your son. I hate you for dying early. I hate you for my lonely years."

Calero, head down, arms on his knees, stared into the clear liquid in the glass he held as Domingo put the cut limes and some salt on the table.

Pulling his chair closer, Domingo continued his lecture. "So you have become like your dog. Kicked in the head, you still chase the hooves that kicked you. If that black stallion hadn't broken free and run away to freedom, Spooky would have long ago been dead. That dog was willing to give his life for one bite at that beautiful black. You admired the dog for that, and now I know why. You are both stupid! You both want what you can't have, and what you can have you don't want."

Calero looked at him. "I've always tried to be a gentleman, Domingo, but after Nola rejected me, I wanted to kill her—visit violence upon her. I had a dream where she taunted me. Then I would walk up to her and spit in her face, and I would feel free, as if I could go on with my life. But, when I'd wake up, once again I'd be tortured by the need to be with her, to touch her, to smell her scent, to feel her hands on me, to look into her eyes…"

"That is the very thing that happened to your father, *Pequeno Mustachio*. 'The Evil One' rejected him because he would not go the way she wanted him to go. He was strong at first and gave her the old macho-man good-bye—'don't let the door hit you in the ass when you leave'—but he couldn't hold it together. She rejected him hard—wouldn't take his calls, had nothing to do with him for days. He made himself sick, didn't want to eat. Finally, he got angry enough to charge at her like a mad bull with its tongue hanging out.

"He went to the Evil One's house, and when she came to the door and looked at him with the cold arrogance of a conquering bullfighter, he drew himself close up to her. Then, looking deep into her eyes, he spit right into her face. After that, he walked away for good."

Domingo sipped some tequila and watched Calero's face. "He told me he knew he was free at last—that he would always be free of the woman. But he lied—to himself. The next thing I knew, he was scheduled to fight in the Tijuana ring, and against some impossible bulls.

"I asked myself why this man would do this, and then I saw her, smiling and touching him. She had control of him. So, he fought *el toro mucho malo*...and he died."

Domingo shook his old head sadly and went on. "Later I learned that after he spit in her face, he went back to her and begged her forgiveness. That was when she caped him even closer to her side and whirled him around. With his head hanging in defeat, she put the sword right into his heart. *Ole! Ole!*

"When I put him in the ground and he had received the hero's burial and all the *ole*'s were said, I turned and walked away and never went back. This was your father's history."

Sighing, Domingo reached across the table and briefly patted Calero's hand. "Our fathers' follies are often destined to be repeated in our own lives, Mustachio. Perhaps it is the destiny of all men to dance too close to the horns because of heartbreak. Your father was a good fighter, but it was your grandfather who was great.

"So the question is, Mustachio, what kind of a man are you going to be—like your father, or like your grandfather? Your grandfather was truly great because he solved the mystery of what it is to be a man." Domingo grew angry. "You, you just dance close to the horns because you think you can get away with it. Well, you have found you can't. The man, as with the bull, always loses. That Nola is the wrong woman for you. Besides, she is not Spanish."

"Domingo! Are you prejudiced? I don't believe it. You love the Mexicans—you sit and tell them stories, you make them honor their culture."

"This woman is not Spanish, she is Mexican—and I think you must have a Spanish woman to avoid what happened to your father. But it is not that Nola is Mexican; it is that she is the Evil One returned. She is the same as the one who was with your father."

Calero threw his arms up. "Jesus Christ, Domingo. Don't give me that Spanish mystical crap. Or is it the Mexican witch-doctors this time?"

"Be assured, Mustachio, this old one knows. She is the one who whispers to come follow her to a new place, away from your own vision. It is a place of domestication, or even death. With her, you are going to be either a steer or one dead bull, my friend.

"I know you are in great pain over this woman. You are bleeding on the inside. Blood comes from the heart, and that's not good. It can be fatal. There are many women who are like the *picador.* They come close to you, they prick and torment, but like the *picador,* they make only superficial wounds. In that way, the bull doesn't bleed from the inside out—it's all on the surface, and never fatal. Tiring and exhausting, but never fatal. But an evil woman, like the one who wants to take your life, goes too far. She wants all of you, will even take the gift of life from you." Domingo swallowed another mouthful of tequila and bit down hard on a piece of lime.

"I can't fight Nola anymore," Calero admitted. "Domingo, I give in to her, and then she dumps me in the shit. When I walk away from her, she lures me back. We go back and forth and there is nothing solid. I become confused, begging for either love or death. I am more and more tired. I can't sleep, and when I do, I dream I'm trapped in the bullring…and the *corrida* music plays over and over."

Feeling sympathy at Calero's confession, Domingo asked, "Does it feel as though your head is too heavy to hold up any more?"

"Yes!" Calero answered him. "Yes, my head hangs down. Sometimes so far I feel my tongue will fall out of my mouth."

"It is that way with the bulls in the ring, Mustachio. Too many pricks and the fight ends. When a woman pricks you many many times, eventually your head hangs down, opening a way through the bone to the heart. It is no longer a game, then, no longer play. It is the murder of a man's soul."

Calero listened patiently as the old man went on. "I see you no longer want to feel the pain of romantic love, Mustachio. It is a love used by the evil *matadora* to lure you onto her sword, my son—not what love is really made of. Real love…life…is made of the stirring of the beans. It is not a pageant of death in the afternoon, the crowds cheering, bands playing. It is the everyday caring—someone bringing you a bowl of refried beans when you are hungry…someone tending to you when you are ill.

"Love is not the *Fiesta Brava.* That is myth, and only fools like your father choose to live in a myth. You must decide whether you want to live a myth or live in the real world. You must decide whether to howl or to bark."

"What?!" Calero interrupted Domingo and sat forward in his chair. "To howl or to bark? What does that mean?"

Domingo, too, leaned forward. "It means I am getting drunk and that soon we will both be very drunk. So drunk we will no longer hear *corrida* music in our minds." Then he poured them both another glass of tequila.

"You hear the music, too?" Calero felt surprise. "The music of the bullring? Tell me, Domingo, do you hear it even when you're awake and not dreaming?"

"Yes, always," he replied. "It is in our Spanish blood. But lately, when I see you, I hear the music that they play when they drag the dead bull out to the butchers."

Calero thought about that for a while, and then he said, "I lost Nola's love and almost blew my brains out over her. I must be crazy."

Domingo spoke softly, "Someday, Mustachio, you will grow strong again—and maybe even wise. The struggle between the bull and the cape—and the magic woman behind it all—are the warring elements which cause you so much suffering, but if you are wise enough, they will not destroy you or bring you to your knees. Then your life can be a work of art and you can become an artist like your *Grande Padre Mustachio.*"

Domingo took another sip of his tequila. "You did the right thing today, Mustachio. You walked out of the ring…left the *matadora* standing in the rain…broke the spell. It will never be this bad again. I know, I have been there, too."

Calero snapped, "I've got to get that bitch out of my life."

Domingo corrected him, "Witch, not bitch. Don't fight her, replace her. Replace her with a good woman. Cancel the *Fiesta Brava.* Don't enter the arena again.

"Mustachio, you should only be with a woman like your grandmother…she who wiped your tears and gave you milk with chocolate in it. When your father teased you for being big and clumsy, she gave you chocolate milk. When he laughed at you for saying you wanted to be a bullfighter, she gave you comfort."

"But, Domingo, I love the excitement I feel at being with Nola…the incredible sex."

"If she was merely a human, you could win. But you've made a goddess of that witch, and she's made you a mindless bull. She will finish you, Mustachio. Remember this picture: Strutting away with her chin held high, an arrogant tilt to her head…and, if she puts you away cleanly enough, she will win both your ears."

Domingo tensed with anger. "Am I sorry for you? No! If you are so deaf you cannot hear the truth, so dumb you just give up, then you deserve to lose your ears. And what difference does it make for you to lose your ears, even your tail, maybe your hooves? You have already lost your *huevos*."

Calero stiffened, anger flashing in his own eyes. "So, you want me to cancel this festival of love? I should walk the *Camino* of the Coward?"

"This is not a festival of love—it is a festival of death. Get that through your head! Can't you see the obvious? She is damaged...scarred...possessed. Study your enemy. Look for the flaws, Mustachio. Be great like *Grande Padre Mustachio*, not weak and blind like your father."

"Domingo, tell me why you've always called me Mustachio. I'm no great fighter. My father told me I was a clumsy nothing, and now I know he was right. Look at me! Kissing *gringos'* asses for a living...having the same nightmare over and over. And I shaved off the mustache." Disconsolate, Calero slumped back in his chair.

"Mustachio, you fought a great fight tonight. Let your mustache grow back. Run from the arena. You cannot win in this woman's game. The gate is open, freedom can be yours. Be like the black stallion—run free!"

Draining his glass, Domingo announced, "I drink no more. It is dawn." He stumbled from the room, fell on his bed, and was instantly asleep.

Calero knew the woman could still win; both he and Domingo knew it. There might yet be a death in the afternoon. Too exhausted to move farther, Calero stretched out on the *casita* floor and he, too, fell asleep.

As they slumbered, a cock crowed, the sun rose, and a new day began.

17

Carmella, Co-conspiritor

For several weeks, Olga had been stopping by Estrellita's Cantina whenever she had the opportunity. She had eaten more authentic Mexican food than she cared to think about, but after her fourth or fifth visit she was accepted as a regular. The Mexican patrons never guessed that the big buxom blonde could understand their rapid-fire Spanish. The men joked about her good looks and attractive big legs, and they never referred to her as a *gringo*.

They had to admire her from a distance, however, since Estrellita would shush up the more graphic of the men if they got out of line with their comments. Estrellita was pleased with Olga. Not only was she a big tipper, but she always wanted to try the best dishes. Unlike some *Norte Americanos*, this big blonde woman was both adventuresome and generous.

In the beginning, Olga would just eat a meal, read the paper, and unobtrusively listen carefully to the Mexican community gossip. Then one day she hit pay dirt.

She heard one of the Mexican women cursing Frank Rodriguez and praising her other employer, the Sinnobar Hills Bank. The woman was telling Estrellita she planned to quit working for "that *hombre* Rodriguez" soon and how she wished she could get even with him in some way. The man had cheated and insulted her.

"Me, Carmella, soon as I have enough money, I return to Mexico with my children," she said in Spanish. "That man is a crook…always having secret meetings in that locked room of his. No one goes in there without him, except me. He thinks I'm stupid and can't read. One man, the head of the bank, I think, goes in there a lot but never alone. Rodriguez doesn't trust him, that's my guess."

When the woman left, Olga called Estrellita over and asked who she was. Could she possibly be looking for work? Cleaning work, perhaps? Estrellita said she would check, and the very next time she saw Olga, she had the cleaning woman's name and phone number for her. She warned her, however, that the woman, Carmella, spoke very little English.

"A good opportunity for me to practice your beautiful language," Olga had responded, and that had pleased Estrellita.

That same evening, Olga called Carmella. *"Buenas noches, Senora Carmella,"* Olga began. Then she went on to speak in perfect Spanish. As their talk continued, trust developed between the two women.

Yes, Carmella would do extra work for *Senora* de Grut, especially if it paid well. Her minimum wages barely kept her family going, and she needed money for four plane tickets. In turn, Olga shared that she had once had a desperate time in Argentina, but now things were good. She could help Carmella and her children.

Quite late into the conversation, Olga asked, "Can you keep a secret, Carmella?"

"Si, mi amiga."

"It is that I have a big problem with that Rodriguez man myself. He is no good. He is like the devil."

Carmella agreed, swore in Spanish and then asked Olga and God to forgive her.

They talked for almost an hour, and as Olga questioned Carmella, she learned more about Frank Rodriguez's mysterious room. The other offices were very grand and exquisitely furnished—especially Mr. Rodriguez's office on the second floor. But not the locked room on the first floor. It had a conference table and chairs, a telephone, and one heavily-curtained window.

The walls were bare except for a huge wallboard that Carmella told Olga she had been warned never to touch. Most of the time, doors were carefully closed over the wallboard, but once it had been left open, and she had seen that it was covered with names and figures. Did *Senora* de Grut really think the information on the board could be useful?

By the end of their conversation, they had arranged to meet at Estrellita's on the following Sunday. Olga asked Carmella to note who visited Rodriguez's office and particularly those who were taken into the locked room.

"Carmella, is there any chance you could write down the names of any people listed on the wallboard in that room?"

"I will try to do it. I must be careful."

"Very careful, dear lady. You already have earned two tickets to Mexico City. Help me a little longer and you will have two more."

Now Olga had her mole, her undercover agent. Carmella was a woman desperate to return to Mexico with her children—a woman with a score to settle and, hopefully, one with an eye for detail.

On Sunday they met as planned, and Olga handed Carmella two tickets to Mexico City. Tears filled the grateful woman's eyes as she spilled out the details of the mystery room—and the four men who met there behind locked doors. She even had the men's names, and that was a shocker for Olga. She watched as Carmella slid a piece of embossed stationery across the table toward her. The fine paper was monogrammed with the letters *FMR*.

"Frank Manuel Rodriguez!" Carmella spoke in the triumphant voice of a *matadora* ready for the moment of truth. Then she slowly read the names listed on the sheet of paper, some of them unexpected names.

Olga couldn't wait to see Newell and tell him about the list. Her hands shook as she folded the sheet of paper and slipped it into her purse. But Carmella had more for her. On one of Estrellita's paper napkins, Carmella made a crude drawing of the mystery room, showing the location of the window and the wallboard directly across from it. How convenient, Olga thought.

The plan for penetration of what Olga thought of as the "mystery room" would require Carmella to somehow leave the door of the incriminating wallboard open and the curtains covering the window facing the street parted an inch or two. That was all Olga would need. Frank's contempt for his so-called uneducated help could cost him dearly.

"All right, Carmella. When you can arrange it, the doors open, the curtains parted, call me at once at this number. Say only this, '*buenas noches, buena vista, listo ahora,*' and hang up."

The conspirators were fast becoming friends—drawn together through their separate needs and a common enemy. Holding each other's hands, their thank yous were plentiful. Caring sisters, united by a potentially dangerous mission— there was no turning back.

Olga's car roared out of the cantina's parking lot as she drove off to use a pay phone she knew of near the Calero ranch. Once there, she dialed 999 and then the rest of the numbers Newell had given her. In a moment, a computer voice instructed her to hang up and wait. Olga impatiently complied.

She jumped when the phone rang. "Newell?"

"Yes, what's up?"

"Got a mole inside what I call Rodriguez's mystery room. Got the names of four schemers for you...you probably need to put a tail on them. They're up to no good...My mole thinks it's all down in black and white. Take down these names."

When he heard the names, Newell whistled. "I can't believe it! These are powerful people. All in it together?"

"I think so. I hope to have the evidence for you soon."

"Be mighty careful. These people will surely be playing for keeps. They could trap and do away with your mole and think nothing of it, you know."

Olga swallowed hard and tried to sound confident. "The mole is under good cover and would never be suspected. She has only one low-risk task to perform," Olga lied, "and then she returns to Mexico with her family—for good."

"You planning to take some calculated risks, Olga? Never mind answering. I'd rather not know what you're planning. Just watch it—you could become a target. Well, this is the break we've needed. Thanks a million." Newell hung up.

Almost immediately the phone rang. Startled from her thoughts, Olga picked it up. "Yes?"

It was Newell, back on the line to say her news had almost made him forget to tell her about the video of the Sinnobar Hill interlopers. It had been analyzed. First, Spooky, the dog, had been tranquilized and was still alive when he was carried off by a fat Mexican kid. The dog had put up a hell of a fight, and they had a good make on the mean guy's mug, the one who kicked the dog. Spooky had bitten him in the ass real bad, and they had a make on that, too. Also, there was another Hispanic, an older man. The other guy was a white man and all business. The video analyst thought he was probably a professional, perhaps a geologist type.

As she listened, Olga picked up the rising excitement in Newell's voice. "But, get this! The tool box that held the high-speed drill and extension bits had some very revealing information painted on its side. It read 'Property of,' now hear this, Olga, 'Triangle Sand and Gravel Company'!" Then, knowing what her reaction would be but not waiting for it, Newell hung up again.

Olga waited five minutes, hoping for more, her heart pounding hard against her chest, but the phone didn't ring again. She was thrilled by the news and by the interesting interconnections that were emerging.

A short time later, after her return to the ranch, Olga felt a little reconnaissance work was in order. Leaving Mary in charge of the office, she got into her car again and drove into town, slowly passing the old bank building that housed the office of Frank Rodriguez. The two-story building was on the corner of Main and Villa, and she turned right on Villa and parked under the last window of the bank facing out on the street.

The old sandstone building looked like a fortress. The window under which she parked began about four feet above the ground and then rose up ten feet to the top of its arch. Drawn blinds covered the bottom of the window and separate curtains covered the semicircular window in the stone arch at the top.

Olga's thoughts were scornful. Fortress and command center, her ass. What a bunch of novices she was dealing with here. It was too easy. A mysterious room on a first floor, its window not blacked out? They probably believe everything's secure about that room because of the bank's alarm system.

Olga thought for a moment and decided all she needed was that curtain left open a couple of inches. Then she'd put old infrared right inside that room—and down their throats. When the camera's pictures were enlarged…Well, she would just have to wait and see.

A secret room without blacked-out security. What arrogance! This Rodriguez clown had set himself up for penetration—deep penetration, proctoscopic penetration. These guys had either a death wish or a stupidity complex. Well, bend over boys, you are about to be penetrated. Piece of cake.

Olga thought again of her Argentina days when security had been her specialty. She could teach these clowns a lot. She had her mole working inside, and hopefully now she was about to get some evidence in black and white.

She planned her next move of the invasion as she drove slowly back to Rancho Calero. She'd need the panel truck, a ladder, some cleaning supplies...Excited at the prospect of what lay ahead, she broke into song, "Don't cry for me, Buenos Aires, the truth is I never left you. All through the old days..."

18

Olga's Cure

Nearing the ranch, Olga thought how she loved it, its people, and Calero. He hadn't seemed himself lately—depressed, riding alone a lot, maybe too much. It was that woman, Nola, she was sure.

The hearings on Rancho Calero were over and they were just waiting for the vote. They had fought hard to keep the riding stable intact even though the city council and county wanted it all under water. The city limits would probably be extended to include the ranch and then it would be condemned for the good of the public. Thirsty Sinnobar Hills and the land developers came before horses, people, and the children.

Well, maybe Calero had given up, but she, Olga, the blonde freight train, backed by the boarders, hadn't. They would march on city hall. Some heads would roll. The "Save Rancho Calero" cell was in high gear planning the operation.

As she drove down the lane, she saw Calero, sitting alone on his horse high on Sinnobar Hill—his favorite place since Nola had dumped him.

The dumb bull of a man just hadn't seen it coming. Nola had seduced him and then dropped him so hard he broke. Calero had run after her like a puppy begging for attention, and he got kicked for it.

God, Olga thought, it makes me so mad I could kill her. He even shaved off that magnificent mustache, started dressing like a city slicker, and was ready to leave the ranch to marry her. Then bang, she puts a fatal bullet through the romance. Well, he was starting to come out of it—slowly. Maybe he would give Karin Noble a chance now. Karin would be good for him—very good. Olga thought she might put Karin's picture up on the office bulletin board.

When Calero saw Olga's car moving slowly down the lane, he shook his head. What would he do without his blonde Argentine general? For the last month she had done everything, while he had struggled each day just to breathe, to survive.

He had been so depressed, so bowed, he'd felt as if some huge weight behind his eyeballs was pushing his face downward—down into the earth. There had been the gritty bitter taste of dust in his mouth that nothing would wash away, not even the large amounts of tequila he'd been drinking. He would wake up choking, gasping for breath, his heart feeling as if it must surely burst. His stomach had been so filled with fear he had wished for a bull to rip out his aching guts on its horns.

Well, he was better now, but so very tired—tired all the time. No get-up-and-go. No interest in any woman—not even the punishing Nola. Not even in the ranch. He felt dead. He had had an ultimate brush with the horns.

It seemed that he was condemned to a life of choosing the wrong woman—a woman who would kill him just as his father had been killed. And he was deeply embarrassed about his actions on that rainy night of his despair.

Would he really have pulled the trigger? Only Domingo knew he had almost blown his brains out over a woman. He still didn't understand it—maybe never would. Was it that he hoped to hurt her by destroying himself, or was he like a bull that runs himself headlong onto the sword just to end the torment, the uncertainty?

Calero perked up a bit as he saw Olga get out of the car and wave to him. She was a good friend. Always trying to help. Loyal to a fault. Nature and time were cruel. Here he was, a Spaniard whose mind, whose very being, was trapped in a body designed more for professional football than the bullring. He hated the game of football.

Ah, but the bullfight—an art form that taught so many lessons. And *Grande Padre Mustachio,* one of the greatest artists of them all. He thought of that grand man caping great and powerful bulls. Oh, to have lived at that time, or to have followed in those slippered footsteps in the sand. But, no, he was a physical throwback, thanks to his mother's Mexican genes. He would have to accept that he was doomed to cape bulls only in his mind. He would never take a turn around an arena ringing with the cheers of the crowd.

It was a hard insight to swallow, and he smiled at the irony of it. He would have to let go of the dreamer Mustachio, retire him, face the fact that he would never be a matador.

He would have to just be himself, whoever that might be. He laughed. Here he was, a dude ranch operator—wouldn't his father be proud! Or should he be a lifeguard at the new expanded lake? That's the ticket, he thought, and throwing his head back, he laughed loud and long.

After that, he felt better and nudged the ever-patient Buck down the hill. It was all about to change—the ranch, the old mansion, he himself. Perhaps it was the new start he needed.

Riding up to the stables, he mused about Karin. They might have made it if the Evil One—he realized it was the first time he'd called Nola that—hadn't come along. Damn, where was his head through all that? He answered himself aloud, "In the arena, stupid! In the arena."

"You are feeling better today, my son," Domingo commented as he took Calero's horse.

Calero grunted and walked slowly to the office. Olga and Mary, already at work, hardly looked up as he entered, but watched as he went to his desk. He saw that the latest *Farm Journal* was open to an article about Karin. There was a picture of her, too—tall, beautiful Karin, standing beside a prize Spanish bull. The headline read, "Karin Noble To Consult With Spanish Government."

Calero looked over at Mary and Olga and caught them as they hurriedly turned back to their work. Women conspiring to help a poor lost soul, he thought, and a smile flickered across his lips.

Through the afternoon the three worked together: Mary, the bouncy optimist; Olga, the efficient general; and Calero, the battered, beaten, but recovering lover of an impossible dream. As the day ended, the women began to talk about the ideal modern woman, the kind of woman who any man with any sense at all would want to marry. A woman like that Karin Noble, for example. Now, there was an ideal one. Warm, beautiful, and educated. A woman who liked being a woman, but who also liked men. A career woman, one who could take care of herself yet want to share...

Calero broke into their comments. "Stop it, you two. I'll call her, I'll call her. I've always liked her, you know...but she probably has someone else by now."

"She liked you, Mr. Calero, she really liked..."

"Mary? Now, how would you like it if I tried to fix you up with the ideal guy?"

"I'd love it!" Mary sputtered. "When? Where? Who?"

While the two bantered, Olga had been busy dialing the phone. Then she spoke. "Hello. Karin Noble? This is Olga out at Rancho Calero. We just wanted to congratulate you on your award and assignment with the Spanish government.

We've been talking about it this afternoon and just had to call. Yes, Mr. Calero is standing by to talk with you, and Mary sends her congratulations, too. I'll put Mr. Calero on. Stand by, please." Olga held the phone receiver in the air as she put the call on hold.

"Damn you two conspirators," he said, but obviously pleased as he reached for the phone.

"Take the call upstairs, *pendejo,*" Olga said.

"Don't mind if I do, ladies," he said with a bow, and then rushed out and up the stairs to his room.

Mary showed her delight. "Olga, he's interested and excited! How do you figure it?"

"Oh, men are like bulls, Mary. There are good ones, bad ones, cowards and brave ones, even great ones. But when it comes to why men choose one woman over another, *Dios solo comprende.* A bull will take any cow, but there a man differs; he is not like that. He may act like he will take any woman, but he won't. When he finds the one he thinks is the only one for him and then loses her, he wants to die. Our *patron* was ready to die for Miss Nola Gag-Me."

"I don't understand it. I've never felt that way."

Olga smiled at Mary's naivete, but answered her seriously. "We will never understand why love can become a demon that devours one's very being. Somehow we lose our protective system, and love can become a cancer that eats us alive."

"What's the cure for it, Olga? For Mr. Calero?"

"Karin." Olga was positive. "Karin Noble is the cure. That fool upstairs is one lucky man to know a woman like her. See how long they've been on the phone? The longer that light stays on, the sooner the cure can take effect—and the less likely that man will relapse."

"Oh, God, Olga, you mean he could go back to Nola?"

"Sure, Mary. He could go back to Nola. Shit happens."

Even after the two women had left for the day, the telephone light still glowed its reassurance that Calero's journey toward a cure was underway.

19

Danger Is My Business

A week passed and with it much of Calero's gloom. He was slowly becoming his old self, no longer looking drawn, sleepless, and preoccupied. And Domingo was looking happier. Olga and Mary winked at each other each time Calero went upstairs to call Karin or to receive her calls. The phone light stayed on long and steady.

On Thursday, Olga worked late, hoping Carmella might call. It was her night to clean Frank Rodriguez's offices. Olga had parked the panel truck near the office, just in case. She had told Calero it was a loaner while her own car was being fixed. She was lost in work when the phone rang. She jumped, took a deep breath, then picked up the receiver and said softly, "Rancho Calero."

"*Senora* de Grut?"

"Yes."

"*Buenas noches, buena vista, muy listo ahora!*" a woman's low conspiratorial voice said. The phone went dead.

Olga sat upright, pulling herself together. "God bless you, Carmella. So it's a good evening, good view, very ready now," she said, translating the message back into the dead phone.

"Camera, action, penetration!" Olga yelled it as she jumped to her feet and rushed to the file cabinet. Grabbing the black camera bag and two magnetic signs she had hidden there, she rushed out to the panel truck. She opened the rear doors and loaded in the bag and the signs. Then she added a tall stepladder and bucket that Domingo, with a questioning look on his face, had obligingly placed beside the truck earlier in the evening. Slamming the doors shut, she locked them, but as she jumped into the driver's seat, she froze.

"Shit!" Bounding out of the truck, she rushed back into the office and retrieved a shopping bag stuffed with clothes. Her first mistake. Better be the last one. Get control. Calm down. No wasted moves, you rusty undercover German. Mentally, she went over her list: camera, signs, clothes, cleaning tools, ladder, bucket. What was needed now was rapid-fire action but calm penetration.

She speeded toward Sinnobar Hills, covering half the thirty-minute drive in ten. Turning the truck into a deserted road, she stopped, jumped in the back and pulled on faded blue coveralls. Pulling her hair back, she tied a red bandana around her head and adjusted wire-rimmed safety glasses. Having finished dressing, she grabbed the two signs, got out of the truck and stuck one up on each side panel. Magnets snapped the signs securely in place, and the truck now belonged to Noches Window Cleaning Company.

The town clock struck eight as she drove down Sinnobar Hills' main street toward her objective. Turning to the right on Villa, she stopped near the mystery room window.

Olga got out of the truck, whistling. She nodded to some passersby, no doubt on their way to one of the many nearby restaurants. There could be no looking around, no checking the surroundings, just a quick efficient window wash by a worker from the Noches Window Washing Company.

Throwing open the back doors of the truck, Olga quickly set up the ladder by the target window, but as she returned to the truck to get the camera, a voice behind her made her freeze.

"Working late, aren't you?" The remark came from a distinguished-looking man standing at the curb just a few feet away.

"That eez what make us different, *senor*," Olga said in an affected Latino voice, all the while sizing the man up out of the corner of her eye. She grabbed a utility belt, strapped it on, and stuffed a squeegee in her back pocket.

"We *muy pronto,* very fast, *senor.* If you want us to do your windows, geeve me your card. We call you about it." Out of the man's sight, she quickly slipped the camera into the bucket, covering it with rags and topping it off with a spray bottle of window cleaner.

"Don't mind if I do," the man said and handed her a card. She slipped it into a breast pocket of her coveralls.

"Please to excuse me, *senor,* I'm behind schedule tonight." Olga brushed past the man close enough to smell his expensive cologne. Reversing the ladder, as if to steady it, she began to climb as the man walked toward the corner. Olga busied herself at the window, but eyed the man suspiciously when he paused and turned. Her heart sank as he started back. Then he stopped, shook his head, and walked off again, disappearing around the corner.

Every fiber of Olga's body had been screaming, 'Don't come back! Don't come back!' Frantically, she cleaned the lower window, then, catching her breath, she climbed farther up the ladder and peered through the small gap in the upper curtains. The room was dimly lit from a nearby street light and she could see a conference table in the almost bare room, and just as Carmella had said, the wallboard. It was in plain sight, doors wide open, ready for old Mr. Infrared.

As Olga reached into the bucket and groped beneath the rags, a light flashed in her eyes. She knew instantly it was the police—she was caught and caught good. She felt as though a bull's horn had hooked her heart, thrown it high into the air, and sent it fluttering down to the sidewalk. The ladder shook and she started to lose control but caught herself.

The patrol car pulled slowly past the panel truck, flashed its spotlight on the truck's sign, and then halted. Olga's hands froze to the top of the ladder. Her mouth was dry, her stomach turned over, and she thought she might faint. She saw the squad car window slide down. "Sorry, sir, just checking," the officer behind the dark glasses said, and just as quickly as they had appeared they were gone.

In a daze, Olga started down the ladder thinking she should find a place to lie down—she was so tired. Still in shock, she looked down and saw the street was deserted.

Then remembrance of what she had set out to do set off an alarm in her brain and energy rushed through her veins. Quickly now, she moved back up the ladder and tore the camera out of the bucket. She didn't waver from her task, even when the precariously perched bucket slipped and fell, banging onto the sidewalk below.

She must be careful now. Balancing the camera firmly, she aimed it through the crack in the curtains. First, she needed a good steady picture of the writing on the wallboard. Then she would have to pan the room, its conference table, the heavy door, then back to the wallboard. By the time it was done, Olga was perspiring heavily. Opening the front of her coveralls, she slipped the camera inside before descending the ladder.

Then she jumped in the truck and drove swiftly off. "I'm too old for this shit!" she was screaming as she sped out of town. Pounding the steering wheel, she willed herself into a rage—at the cops who had frightened her, at the asshole who had given her his card. Groping in her breast pocket, she felt for the card and pulled it out. Turning on the dome light, she read what it said: Jackson P. Busterud, President, Sinnobar Hills Bank and Trust Company.

Olga was crying as she pulled off the road into a parking area and climbed into the back of the truck to change her clothes. When she had changed, she tore the magnetic signs off the sides of the truck and threw them in the back. Then she walked slowly to the edge of the parking area. It was on a hill road that looked down into the valley toward the twinkling lights of Rancho Calero. With her tears gone, she screamed out into the valley, "Yes!" and heard the valley echo back her cry.

Before she walked back to the truck, she took one last look at the distant lights and said softly, "The condemned shall become the condemnors, and the abusers reap abuse unto themselves. So saith Olga de Grut."

20

How Much for the Penthouse?

Karin and Calero sped along Highway 17 toward the town of Santa Cruz. The high noon sun was hot on the hood of the pickup, and Joe cursed the Chevy dealer for not fixing the air-conditioning right. He slid open the back window and the flow of air gave some relief.

Glancing over at Karin, he saw her looking intently at the two stone cats that graced the entrance to Colonel McPearson's hidden mansion. They passed by the stone cats quickly and Calero saw them reappear in his rearview mirror. Those large carved cats had given the nearby town its name—Los Gatos.

His mind drifted back to the incompetent mechanic and to Santa Cruz just over the mountain. "Santa Cruz is a place I hate," he had told Karin. "It's filled with hippies and dopers who should be scooped up and sent to Alaska to build igloos."

But Karin had shared that she loved the place, and she had coaxed, "Come on, Calero, let's go to Santa Cruz. Just you and me. It's not that bad. There are a lot of free spirits there, but they're interesting, Calero. They're like you—weird, strange…bent by the winds of some other time…You know, so many people are poorly defined—no curves, no scars or wrinkles. They're just plain blah. I find the characters in Santa Cruz unique, different…they excite me."

Calero's glance took in her body, and he thought, "I sure love her curves. What I can't accept is that she seems to have no flaws or scars. Could it be that this slender woman, with the curves that please me so, is really just a normal healthy person in this scarred world? How can I trust my feelings when I was so blind about Nola? Look out, *matador*...the unseen hook of a horn can be fatal."

Yet, there she was, with long blonde hair pulled tight and wound into a knot behind her head. Calero had wondered what it would be like if she let her hair down. She wasn't ready to do that yet, but she was ready to go to Santa Cruz.

They arrived in the early afternoon, walked out on the wharf, and had something to eat. They talked, watching passersby and seagulls, and then they became aware that the sun had began to set.

"You know, it's so beautiful here I wish we didn't have to go back home," Karin mused as they walked out to the end of the pier to be closer to the setting sun.

"Then why go back?" Calero said.

Karin looked a little startled. "You mean stay?"

"I'll stay if you will...and if you promise not to take advantage of me, I promise not to take advantage of you."

"You've got a deal," she said playfully. "I love that idea. We could get a place with twin beds."

"Exactly what I had in mind." Calero grinned back at her.

But Karin looked doubtful. "The great Calero, the great Spaniard, without any intentions?"

"At my riding stables, my beautiful one, there are over a hundred women who come and go. Have any of them ever said I took advantage of them?"

"Oh, no, no. I've heard some of them say you are always a gentleman, a perfect Spanish gentleman."

"I shall be a gentleman. Whatever happens is up to you. You will set the rhythm of our time together."

Karin threw her arms around him and spun him around.

Calero, in his proud way, didn't move too fast but let her pull him just a little, a little closer in the direction he truly wanted to go. To bed.

Karin grabbed his arm. "Come on. I know an inexpensive place where we can stay. They have twin beds and it won't cost very much. We can have dinner in a little deli that's right next door."

Calero looked at her warmly. "If we are going to stay here, we must stay where we can hear the ocean, and in a place both of us will never forget."

Karin frowned. "You've stayed here before!"

"No, never. You don't understand. I told you. I don't like Santa Cruz. It's filled with strange people bent in strange ways."

"Then where do you think we should stay?"

Calero looked off across the water and saw a beautiful, expensive-looking hotel rising above the beach. High on top of the building were penthouses with peaked roofs. He pointed. "I think we should stay there. High above the hippies and the smell of marijuana. Up there where the birds go to breathe."

"Calero! That'll cost a fortune. We can't stay there."

"We are going to stay there and listen to the ocean. If I have to sleep alone, I want a wonderful view and I want to hear the ocean, and I don't want any rooms above me. Most of all I want to be high enough so that everyone down below looks well-dressed."

"Okay. Listening to you, I find I want the same thing you do."

Moments later, as he drove up in front of the hotel, Calero said, "I can't believe this place is called The Dream Inn. Wait in the car, Karin, while I check the place out."

Once inside, he walked up to the registration desk. "How much for the penthouses, the ones with the peaked roofs?"

The clerk eyed Calero doubtfully. "I'm not sure we have one available."

"You have one available. How much are they?"

"Three-fifty a night."

"Okay, we'll stay a week. If the service and everything else is excellent, me and the missus may stay a month."

"A month?" the attendant gasped.

"Yes, a month. Will the suite be available for that time?" Calero pulled two twenty-dollar bills from his wallet.

"Yes, sir. We could even give you a special price...let me just check the records, sir. The corner unit is available...that's the presidential suite. Usually four hundred fifty dollars...but two hundred fifty dollars a night will do just fine. We'd like you to try it."

"I'm sure you would. We'll take it." He folded the twenties and slipped them under the registration pad.

Riding up in the elevator, Karin slumped against him. "You really are magnificent, *senor Don* Calero."

He felt himself becoming aroused, but he wasn't going to do anything about it. This was her time. He noticed his heart was beginning to beat hard against his chest.

Later, as the moonlight softly lit up the night, he opened the sliding glass door to the balcony of their room and heard the waves below splashing in and out, in and out.

Lying back on one of the luxurious beds, his arms folded behind his head, he waited, and waited. He felt calm and peaceful, and the air smelled good as it flowed into the room through the open balcony door. Karin was in the bathroom, and his heart pushed hard against the wall of his chest with anticipation. Then she came into the room and stood at the end of the bed.

"I've come to say good night, *Don* Calero."

"I know." He smiled.

Then she was on the bed, kneeling at his feet. Her hands reached out and began to move slowly, seductively, up his legs—pushing against his feet, his calves, and up his thighs. By the time she reached the edge of his shorts, he was screaming inside with the desire to move, his heart pounding with such force he thought he would die. Yet, he lay there without moving.

She edged forward, gripped his shorts and began to pull at them. As she freed him, her tongue came against his member and licked. Calero was so stirred he thought he would die from the ecstasy of it. At the same time he kept thinking control, control…control.

Lifting herself away from him, Karin slid past his erect penis to kiss him on the mouth. Gripping him in her hand she was murmuring, "Oh, Jesus, if only we hadn't made a deal, I'd screw you to death, you beautiful Spaniard!" Then she was gone, into the other bed, and almost immediately she was asleep.

Calero lay there in absolute amazement, watching his member slowly recede against the shimmering light coming through the window and whispered, "That is one unusual lady."

Unable to sleep, he began thinking about his life and some of the things he had gone through. He thought about the deal he had made with Karin and he knew that he could break it. Two feet away was a beautiful, desirable woman, and he could take advantage of her, but he would not. On that thought, he drifted off to sleep and woke to find bright sunlight streaming into the room.

He looked across the room, but Karin wasn't in her bed. Had he disappointed her? Had she left? Where was she? The bedside clock said it was almost ten. How had he slept so well? Then he heard the bathroom door open, and Karin came out dressed in a clinging white satin slip.

"It's a new day, *Don* Calero," Karin announced. "All previous deals and contracts are off."

Calero watched as she came to him again at the foot of the bed. The night before began to repeat itself. It ended with her sitting on top of him, slowly moving up and down, her hands pressed against his chest while she pleaded, "Please don't move…please don't move, please, please…stay still, stay still." Then she moved her hands down, and bringing the satin slip over her head, she tossed it aside. She still had her bra on. Self-conscious about her breasts? He knew they must be beautiful but he made no move to free them. She began to move up and down again. "Don't move. Don't move…please, please…"

Feeling he could explode inside her, he kept warning himself, "No, don't do that to her. Let her do what she needs to do."

She began to move faster, sliding up and down on his steadily erect member, and much as he wanted to move around and around and meet her body, he lay still.

When she stretched behind her back and began to fondle him, Calero's control slipped, and reaching up, he circled his hands around her breasts and loosed them from the confining bra. Then, reaching around her back, he unhooked the bra and her breasts fell free. They were bouncing as she moved up and down, up and down. Reaching up again, he released her hair. The last thing he noticed, as golden hair tumbled down over her shoulders, was how the morning sun sparkled through it. Then he gave himself up to the ecstasy.

Later, as he piled the pillows up and straightened the bed, he propped himself against the headboard and wondered what Karin, this all-American girl with the slender body, would like for breakfast. "I just bet it's not *huevos rancheros*," he mused. He could hear Karin moving about in the bathroom as he picked up the phone and dialed room service.

"Mr. Calero in the presidential suite here. Please send up the following, and you might want to write all this down...one continental breakfast, one order scrambled eggs and bacon, one order eggs over easy with fried potatoes, juice—one orange, one grapefruit, a large bowl of fresh mixed fruit...and enough coffee for four. Oh, yes, one filet mignon, broiled rare and thinly sliced. Please repeat that order back to me." He listened briefly, then added, "Thank you, and one more thing—an ice-cold glass of milk—in your tallest and best stemware."

As he hung up, Karin, fresh from her shower, popped out of the bathroom. "You decent, my handsome man?" Bounding onto the bed, wet hair and all, she kissed him playfully on the mouth, and then handed him a large towel. "Please help me dry my hair, *senor.*" He felt aroused again but did as she asked, and as he did, they listened to the waves whispering onto the beach below them and to laughter of children in the distance. Each was absorbed in the gentle turning of their own thoughts.

Karin finally spoke. "You are a very keen observer, my friend. I absolutely lost myself back there...you know, the self that's always telling me to be careful, to watch myself. It just disappeared." She wriggled comfortably. "I felt so free and safe—even though the keenest of observers was watching and experiencing my every move. Why, I wonder? Is that what it is to be truly cared for?"

Calero sighed. "Karin, I often see things in ways no one else sees them. It can be a curse...but it diminishes to nothing when I'm with you. Then I feel an unsettling joy I've never known before. A joy...a deep happiness...I can't put what I feel into words, Karin."

Her hand reached out to cover his, and in the silence that followed, Calero heard again faint strains of *corrida* music. "I want to tell you something about myself, Karin. Domingo says I'm like my grandfather, *Grande Padre Mustachio.* He was the only bullfighter to do the Pacheco Pass with the cape…over and over again…and live. Domingo says he was successful because he missed nothing, not even the swing of the bulls' testicles."

Calero sighed again. "He employed such skill in the bullring; I only seem to get myself in trouble. I would have loved to be a bullfighter, too, Karin…yet here I am—nothing but a dude ranch operator pandering to horse-crazy *gringos*."

"Shush," Karin told him as she put her finger to his lips. "You're my hero, so you can't say anything negative about yourself, *Don* Keen-Observer."

"Like the bull, we all, men and women, do the same thing, Karin. We turn toward the damage. Always trying to protect, or correct, or avoid the past…and so, perhaps, we are doomed."

"Why is that?" Karin said, as she sat up and looked full at him.

"I'm not a wise man or a psychologist, Karin, but Domingo says *Grande Padre Mustachio* realized that fighters injured in the ring seemed destined to repeat a pattern that leads them to disaster. The harder they try not to repeat their history, the quicker they play out their destiny. That is why, so often, the horn always rips the same path through their bodies. Our scars, our wounds, our sorrows…they are like the music of the *corrida*. Like it, they draw our attention, pointing the way, inviting the horn."

"Oh, my sweet Joe," Karin said as she touched his face. "Which way do you turn? Toward your pain or away from it?"

"Me? Ah, yes, me. I shall tell you because you are Karin, the one without scars, the one who is perfect because she is not damaged."

"Shush. Tell me, which way do you turn, my sweet love?"

"I turn inward, always inward…inward."

Karin reached out to him, laying her hand over his heart. "I always knew there was something…something like that, but I didn't think you would ever tell me. Thank you for sharing yourself with me. I shall never tell anyone, my brave love." She turned away slightly to hide a sympathetic tear in her eye, and seeing it, the 'keen observer' smiled and loved her all the more.

A tap on the door broke their mood. "Mr. and Mrs. Calero? I have your breakfast."

"Good," Calero said. "Now we will have the Breakfast of Champions."

"Wonderful…I'm starved." Karin leapt from the bed, spun a sheet about her body sarong-style and bolted over to the door.

Laughing, Calero struggled to cover himself with what was left of the bed linen.

21

The Verdict Is In

"Hey…Colonel! Hey, Colonel. San Jose News," said the young man, identifying himself. "How much money did you guys win in there?"

The colonel stopped and faced the small group of reporters. "Sorry, son, I'm not at liberty to tell you how much the jury awarded Miss Julie."

"Can you tell us anything?" another voice interrupted.

"Yes, I can. My name is Colonel Melbourne C. McPhearson and I can tell you what the 'C' in my name stands for."

"Well, okay, if that's important. What does the 'C' stand for?"

"Son, it stands for Cash, and we got Miss Julie an awful lot of cash in there."

The other reporters jumped in and began firing questions.

"Did you come out of retirement for your piece of the settlement?" a young woman asked, a sarcastic inflection in her voice.

"No, young lady, I did not. I came out of a very comfortable retirement as a matter of honor. A fine woman's world was under siege, and honor required I break that siege and bring peace and justice to her world again. We did just that…and placed the sword of southern justice where it would do the most good," he drawled dramatically.

"Got them in the wallet while they were bending over the trough of greed, huh, sir?" a reporter piped up.

"Such a beautiful way to put it, son. Could have used you in there when I was doing the summation. Might have gotten another million or two."

"How much did you get?" they chorused. "Come on."

The colonel held up his hand for silence.

"With all due respect for your jobs, the case will undoubtedly go up on appeal because of the size of the punitive damages. Therefore, I must reserve further comment for a later date. But, I can tell you that Miss Julie has got Cash, and that is my middle name, on her side. And, it has been said that Cash begets cash."

"Well, I'll be a son of a bitch!" The voice came from the edge of the crowd. "Cash! His middle name is Cash! Goddamn it, Olga, did you know all along that he was a member of the Cash family?" Calero was wide-eyed.

"Of course, Mr. Keen-Observer. The grandson of Judge Cash, to be exact. Besides, Argentine cops know everything, *pendejo.* That silver-haired old fox came out several times to the ranch, watching everything you did to improve and restore it. While you were busy being a gentleman from yesteryear, giving away horses to kids and throwing down your jacket so the beautiful woman wouldn't have to step in the mud, I was watchin' and doin' what was important.

"I could see that fine gentleman had something on his mind, so I asked him one day why he cared so much about Judge Cash's old mansion. When I saw tears in his eyes and he talked about his mama and his granddaddy, I knowed…"

"Come on, Olga, where'd you learn to talk like that?"

"Just as soon as I saw the tears in the colonel's eyes, I knowed we had us a friend. He told me he used to be a judge in this county before he retired ten years ago. About that time, I was beginning to realize we might need a judge and attorney here who wasn't owned by the Triangle Sand and Gravel Company."

"Boy, oh boy! If you didn't look so much like a German war camp guard, you might be able to pull off that southern belle routine and marry that grand old man."

"You wait until you see me at the hoedown. You're going to see a real southern belle, and I may just have one fine former judge as my escort."

Calero put his arm around Olga, "You know, I just love the way you work. You got a job for life, Olga."

"How about a partnership?"

Calero stared at the forthright woman. She's serious, he thought. "Okay, Olga, you can have it any way you want."

"Good," she said, snapping open her big black purse and pulling out some papers. "Take a look at this partnership agreement the colonel drew up in his spare time. Lot of advantages for you in it, like free time to travel. You can always use me as the bad guy—keep you from giving the Rancho away. With you out of the way, these German hands can get some real work done."

Calero was speechless. Olga was always one step ahead of him and never seemed to miss a play.

"Another thing. I want you at the parade within the hour. The boarders deserve it, the Save Rancho Calero Committee expects it, and your new partner requires it."

Batting her eyelashes, she added in a thick southern drawl, "We'd be much obliged if you got your Spanish ass there on time, *Don* Calero, y'all. See ya."

He watched her waltz away and felt a deep warm love that somehow made him feel secure and safe.

"Mr. Calero, Mr. Calero," Mary yelled, pushing her way through the milling crowd. "Wasn't it just great in there?"

"Yes, Mary, it was great theater and the colonel was certainly a star. He was like *Grande Padre Mustachio* doing the Pacheco Pass, drawing the bull close, and then the clean precise kill. Those bastards will never get up! Never!"

"And those slick San Francisco attorneys were no match for the colonel, Mr. Calero. They should never have insulted Miss Julie while she was on the stand—referring to her by her first name and looking down their noses. Big mistake." Mary shook her head. "Colonel McPhearson won a lot of points, too, when he said, 'Your Honor, I don't wish to enter a formal objection, but I would like to say to learned counsel, and to you most humbly,'—oh, I loved that part the best—'that I request counsel refer to my client as Miss Davis. We'd be most obliged if Miss Davis could be so respectfully addressed.' Then he bows. It was just the greatest!…I think I may become an attorney, Mr. Calero."

"You'd make a fine attorney, Mary, or an actress for that matter. Give you some white hair and put you in a white suit, and you could be the colonel himself. Coffee?"

"No, thanks. Got to get ready for the Rancho Calero victory parade."

"What made you think we would win that battle?"

"Olga said so…and she's always right. Besides, with what came out in that trial, I'd say some of your enemies are going to end up in the joint." Mary gave him a surprise peck on the cheek and darted off.

Calero began walking toward the park. He needed time to absorb what had just happened. The colonel and Miss Julie had won the case against the Farley Real Estate Company, and the jury had awarded heavy punitive damages. The colonel had convinced the jury that Farley had switched papers on Miss Julie and that she had no intention of selling the Santa Clara homestead. And the buyers of the property—

Frank Rodriguez, et al—they had dirty hands up to their armpits, too.

The infrared photos taken inside Frank's office put the
finishing touch on the case. The clear detailed photographs
looked as though they had been taken by a real professional.
Olga had even been willing to go to jail for the photographs.
Carmella and her children had returned safely to Mexico, so
only Olga had been at risk—she believed the risk was worth
it—and so it had been.

The park was almost deserted. Calero took a seat close to
the street and began musing. The colonel was a great matador. With amazing grace and balance, he had made a tough
job look easy—the mark of a true professional. He drew the
enemy close, and when he could have put him away, he paused
and rested him. The bastards thought they could win, and so
they charged again and again. The audience—the judge, the
jury, and the gallery—had held their breath and prayed for
the colonel to win.

Calero smiled to himself as he thought of the atmosphere
in the courtroom. He had almost seen and heard the pounding hearts, had smelled the ozone in the air like when lightning
strikes.

The moment of truth. Those photographs. Those huge,
bigger-than-life photographs, with their evil scheming plan
of destruction, were so large that people in the back of the
courtroom could read all the names of places listed for acqui-
sition. The priorities had been clearly listed: (1) Davis
homestead, (2) Rancho Calero, (3) Sinnobar Hill. Partners—
Frank, Don, Jackson and George. High in the right hand
corner, in legible handwriting, had been the word "elimi-
nate" followed by the name Joe Calero. A chill ran through
Calero as he recalled the X scrawled across his name—an
angry black, slashing mark of death.

He tried hard not to think about that sword, that rusty piece of steel that had almost taken his life at the De la Cruz exit off the freeway. The memory of that event had come flooding back when he saw the *X* scrawled through his name. They really had tried to kill him.

Yes, Frank Rodriguez, I know the sword was meant for me. Calero nodded to himself. But, tell me, Frank, how big a part did your sister play in all of this? When she couldn't kill me in the bullring of love, when she couldn't torture me until I killed myself, did you decide to do it for her? And, Domingo, you were right. The evil one returned from the grave to claim yet another victim, another Mustachio.

Frank, as a boy, must have been like the jet-skiing kid with the chipped tooth. An irresponsible delinquent with no conscience to warn him about the dangers of doing wrong. When *Don* Rodriguez, his strict and controlling father died, there was no one to guide and discipline Frank, the delinquent, so he blossomed into Frank, the criminal—a power-hungry, wealthy man controlling a sand and gravel empire and the city of Sinnobar Hills. If I hadn't stopped him, he wouldn't have hesitated to kill me.

Nola was another case, he thought, his pulse quickening, his groin tingling. A smart and responsible person like her father—basically ethical, I think. Frank manipulated her, that's all. She may end up in jail, and maybe I could save her. Why do I care? She's the evil one returned. Why do I twist my being, believing I could help her? She wanted me dead; at one point I almost killed her. Anger filled him then, and the sensation in his groin disappeared.

His thoughts turned to the trial, and he laughed at how the colonel had really kicked ass. "You didn't truly represent the two sisters, those wonderful pillars of the community, did you, Mr. George Farley? You manipulated them," the colonel had roared, walking nearer to the sweating witness. "Mr.

George Farley, you represented the buyer, and the buyer was you, isn't that correct, sir?"

"No...I represented him." Farley had pointed weakly toward Frank Rodriguez as a collective gasp rose from the gallery. Farley, slumped in the witness chair, had accented each word after that with a pointing accusative finger. "He made me do it! He made me switch the appraisal papers for a contract of sale." Then, turning to Miss Julie, he'd cried out, "I'm so...sorry, Miss Julie, so..." That's when he had dissolved into tears and sobbed the courtroom into adjournment.

"Yes, the devil made him do it," the colonel had whispered to the jury, leaning in close, his eyes filled with wisdom. "We have no further questions, do we?"

Calero opened his eyes and felt the warm sun on his face. He was drained but happy.

"Mommy, Mommy, look, a parade!" A little boy went yelling past, running toward the street with his mother in hot pursuit.

From down the street the Sinnobar Hills High School Marching Band came round the corner and headed toward Calero and the park. Jumping up, he couldn't believe his eyes. There was this big woman dressed in tights, short red pleated skirt, white boots, and red hat, and pumping a marshal's long golden baton. He couldn't quite make out who it was, but he knew damn well he wouldn't be attracted to her.

On they came, and as they closed in on him, a crowd began to gather. "Holy shit!" he said under his breath as he recognized the woman with the baton. It was Olga de Grut, pounding the pavement in front of the band.

"Mama, what does the sign say?" A child standing next to him pulled on her mother's sleeve.

"The sign says 'SAVE RANCHO CALERO FOR THE CHILDREN.'"

"Mama! Look, here come horses! Can I ride, mama? Can I?" The child begged, doing a universal children's dance of joy.

Calero made his way into the street as Olga came strutting toward him, her ample German thighs testing the tights she was wearing. He rushed up to her and gave her a big hug, whirling her around. "You look beautiful, honey. Just keep marching, just keep on marching for the kids," Calero said, and then turned to go back to the sidewalk.

"I will, *pendejo*," she yelled above the blare, and gave him a big goose that sent him scooting back into the crowd.

He watched her strut out of sight, looking closely at her disappearing figure. Maybe I could fall...nah. Maybe sleep just one time...nah. She does look pretty good and...nah. Come on, Calero, she's your partner and she's a damn fine friend.

22

Showdown/Hoedown

"Smell that, Newell? Man, oh, man, they must be cooking ribs the other side of the lake." The older of the two black men fishing the lake licked his lips appreciatively. "Like to get me some, but the big 'Mex' man is a hardass on fishermen. Kicked my butt off his property. Said I was tresspassin'. I likes the other side the lake—lot of women there sittin' on those big horses 'n gettin' turned on."

Newell wasn't listening to Benford's babble. Lost in the peace of the setting sun, his eyes sleepily followed his fishing line out to where the water shimmered gold and red. It didn't matter that he hadn't caught any fish, he was just happy being at the lake. Happy to hear sounds of music and people laughing, and happy to be with his old friend, Benford. Across the lake, he could see the mansion and watched as its windows glowed crimson from the setting sun, and then went dark. Moments later, they twinkled to life again as someone turned the lights on inside the house.

The music sounded good drifting across the lake. Ordinarily he didn't care for Mexican music, but this was different. *"Mariachi,* I think they call it. Pretty." He was unaware he had spoken his thoughts aloud until he heard Benford's voice.

"What?" Benford said. "What'd you say?"

"It was the music. I said it was pretty."

"Yeah," said Benford, "sure is." Staring across the lake, he added, "What say you 'n me dump our poles and jive on over and get us some o' them goodies?"

"Pussy or ribs?" Newell asked.

"Both." Benford looked hopeful.

"Suppose they just happen to notice we're black?" said Newell.

"Then tell 'em you're a cop and I'm your deputy."

"Well, I may be a cop, Benford, but they'll know right away you're a garbage collector."

"How they gonna know that?"

"By the smell!" Newell laughed as he reeled his line in from the darkening water. "I can just see their noses turning up."

"You go ta hell, Newell. Let's go. Be excitin'. They's all drinkin' and eatin'. See, we sneak around the lake and…"

"No, we don't sneak. We drive in just like we've been invited."

"And get our asses kicked?"

"Cops don't get their asses kicked. Let's go, it's getting dark. There'll be no showdown at the old hoedown tonight, so don't worry. Just follow my lead and you won't get your black ass kicked."

"Better be right," Benford muttered. He scurried after Newell, who was halfway to the black Ford pickup truck parked by the side of the road.

The two sped through the hills surrounding Calero Lake as the sun nestled itself behind the Gabilan Range. They quickly arrived at the spot where huge white painted rocks marked the entrance to Rancho Calero. Tall white border fences served to herd the celebrants and aim them toward the ranch house and its festival in full swing.

A hundred yards down the road they saw the sign stretched overhead: ANNUAL CALERO HAYRIDE AND BARN

DANCE—GUESTS ONLY. Then they saw the soldiers with guns.

Benford grabbed at Newell's arm. "Stop, Newell! Turn around! They got guns!"

Ignoring the protests from his worried companion, Newell kept driving toward the heavyset guards, bandoleers across their chests and weapons at the ready.

"Let's tear right through them and dust 'em good!" Newell said, glancing sideways at his friend and stepping on the gas. Then he heard Benford gulp audibly. "Relax, Benford, they just look mean. I'll just drive past them real fast. Watch this."

"No-o...Newell! Dammit, don't be stupid...son of a bitch!"

Newell obligingly backed off on the accelerator, came to a respectable stop at the gate, and lowered both windows.

"*Alto!*" a tough-looking man came up to Newell's window and ordered, "What's the password?" The other guard pushed his meaty face into Benford's open window and sneered at him.

"Olga sent me," Newell said, staring at the guard through narrowed eyes.

Immediately, a broad smile crossed the man's face. Now it expressed open friendliness. "*Bienvenito, compadres. Passe inmediatamente. Tiene una cerveza para me.*"

"*Con su permiso? Tal vez dos cervezas, mi amigos,*" Newell replied, and his glance took in the man's bandoleer. "Great outfit! See you later at the party." And Newell drove on down the dusty lane.

"Well, kiss my...Who's Olga?"

"Aha! A very special friend, Benford. But not your type."

"Yeah...like those killers back there. Wonder the bastard on my side didn't blow my head off. Biggest barrel I ever saw. They shouldn't be allowed to have guns like that."

As Newell drove on, the music got louder, and parked cars thickened along the side of the road. Just before the lane hooked, there was a sign: PARK HERE.

"Better do it, Newell. There's another dude with a gun. We ain't gonna get out of this alive unless that Olga what's-her-name's got some clout."

The man with the gun came up to them. *"Alto!* Out! *Andale!* Hurry up, or you'll miss the stagecoach." The gunman pushed Newell and Benford toward a waiting Wells Fargo stagecoach, its horses stomping restlessly.

Waving to kids sitting on top of the coach alongside a guitar player, the two men piled inside and closed the door. The horses strained forward, and up top the children began singing "La Bamba." The other couple in the coach sang along. Benford relaxed a little and Newell smiled broadly.

Five minutes later they arrived in what seemed to be the center of the cowboy-party universe. A view of a huge barbeque pit swirled in and out of drifts of delicious-smelling smoke. Cowboy cooks in tall chefs' hats surrounded an enormous chief chef standing right in the center of things— smiling, chatting, and serving up the food.

Benford leaned out the window to enjoy the sight of the house, the straw bales outlining the dance floor, joyous children running everywhere, and most especially, the pretty women in old-fashioned Western and Mexican dress. Suddenly it all disappeared, blocked out by a weathered mustachioed face, so close the features were blurred. Benford jerked his head inside the stagecoach and whispered, "Jeez! Another gunman!"

The doors to the coach were jerked open, and Benford's gunman said in a gentle voice, "You folks can get out now."

As they left the stagecoach, Newell steered Benford to what appeared to be the center of the party. Suddenly, a squeal pierced the evening, and through the crowd pushed Olga de

Grut, nudging people aside with her bustling hoop skirt. Throwing her arms around Newell, she spun him around and planted a big kiss smack on his mouth. "Finally, you've come." Benford stared, his mouth open.

"All this began with you, Newell. If it hadn't been for you…if it hadn't been for the infrared cameras you lent me…"

"Sh-h. Remember, Olga, professional courtesy requires silence and secrets."

"Oh, bullshit! This is America, not Argentina. In Argentina you'd already be dead. They would have shot you for making passes at me, let alone for giving me that equipment."

"That may be, Olga, but I still need to preserve my job here."

Olga ignored Newell's confidential air and began pulling him by the hand to the head of the chow line. "Beer, beer for my friends! Calero, he's here!" She paused for breath. "Come on, come on. You want ribs? You want chicken…steak?…whatever you want.

"Come on! Come on! You, too, cutie-pie." Olga motioned in Benford's direction. "Come meet Calero! Come meet my boss.

"*Don* Calero, may I present Mr. Infrared Newell himself. You can call him Newell."

Newell flushed. "Sh-h, Olga, please don't."

Calero smiled. "*Mucho gusto en conocerlo. Me casa es su casa.* Or, may I say, my rancho is your rancho."

"*Gracias, Don* Calero. It's a pleasure to be here and a pleasure to meet you at long last."

"The pleasure is mine, *Senor* Newell. Ribs, chicken, steak, or all three?"

Newell selected ribs and Benford, ignoring the frown from Newell, took all three.

Calero served them some corn and beans. "How is it you know Olga?" he asked Newell

"Let's just say I was able to help her out once and that's why she invited me to this party. Certainly be happy to pay for big-eater Benford and myself. This shouldn't be on the house."

"No, no, *senor.* Permit me. You are my guests and Olga's friends. *Cerveza?*"

Newell requested Dos Equis.

"And what's your name, pardner?" Calero asked, towering over Benford.

"You can just call me Benford."

"You in the same business as Mr. Infrared?"

"Actually, I work for BFI," mumbled Benford, one eye on Olga, who had just come over to them.

"Did you say BFI? Is that like the FBI, Benford, or what?" asked Olga through a vino haze, standing close and taking his arm.

"Well…BFI sort of has to do with picking up garbage."

"Isn't it the truth? Dammit. Same kind of work I was doing in Argentina. It's just like picking up garbage, isn't it, Benford?"

"You got that right. Day after day, picking up garbage. Pick it up, throw it in the bucket…"

Benford paused as he saw Newell roll his eyes and Calero wink.

Unaware, Olga picked up the conversation. "I like a man knows the score. Pack that food away, honey, and some more beer…get a little heat on to catch up to me. When that band comes on, we'll show them cowboys a little 'southern' soul-dancing."

Newell and Benford, shortly after that, were dragged by Olga to a table covered with a red and white checkered table cloth. It was near the dance area and was lit by a red hurricane candle. Nearby, a band tuned up at the entrance to the barn. Children frolicked on the dance floor while their parents, lost in the delights of chili beans, corn on the cob, and barbequed meats, let them play uninterrupted.

As the twilight deepened, the red emergency light mounted on the wall behind the western band was now casting a friendly, theatrical glow.

The *mariachis* had been moving among the tables playing requests, and Calero brought all ten of them to Newell's table. "A song for my friends, *me amigos. 'La Rieiera,' por favor.*" Leaning down, Calero explained, "In English, that means 'The Soldier's Woman.'"

Calero moved on then, going from table to table greeting his guests and introducing himself to new friends. He was the unassuming hero of the day. As he passed by, people whispered the news, "This isn't just the annual Rancho Calero barbeque party—it's a victory celebration. Rancho Calero won't be flooded and that wonderful man has a twenty-five-year lease to boot...Our grandkids will be riding here. Heard he kicked the county's butt." So it went. The good news followed Calero around the arena as he saluted the crowd, feeling not a hero but a rescuer of dreams.

The colonel was there, standing on the front porch, lost in thoughts of the past. "More sherry, Colonel?" It was Mary, standing behind the screen door with a silver tray.

"My, you look like something out of bygone days in that long white frock," he said, opening the door for her.

"Thank you," she said and executed a bit of a curtsy. "Olga got it for me." She filled his glass with the special sherry Calero had ordered. The colonel smiled and then asked her, "Who's the man talking with Domingo?"

"Oh, that's Dr. Parker. He was one of the first boarders here. He came about ten years ago, that's why Mr. Calero knows him so well. He has an Arabian mare named Paisana and she's very well trained."

As the colonel watched from the porch, Sidney Parker and Domingo leaned against Domingo's *casita*, sipping their beers. They appeared deep in conversation.

Parker was using the opportunity to thank Domingo for his help, and Domingo had replied, "And for yours."

"There's always a danger," said Parker, "from the inside and from the past. It's all inside us, isn't it, Domingo? Even the temptress with the cape."

"The evil ones always come back," Domingo said, nodding his head.

"I can't believe it's been so many years since I first came down that lane. We didn't trust one another then, did we?"

Domingo looked thoughtful. "Our worlds were too far apart. No?"

"Yes. I remember how I hated bullfighting and how you loved it."

"For a Spaniard to hate bullfighting would be to hate life." Domingo looked at Parker, who seemed lost in thought.

All the fundamental forces of nature are trapped in a stupid animal, Parker was thinking, and when he is pricked and prodded he turns into a raging beast with tunnel vision. There is the stamp of the human foot, the cry of *"toro, toro,"* followed by the headlong, head-down charge of all those bundled, primitive forces. My god!

The last section of the orange ball of the sun was just dropping behind Sinnobar Hill when Nola Rodriguez came roaring up to the fiesta in her Alante, throwing out a billowing cloud of dust.

"Hey, you! Slow down!" several voices screamed in unison.

Nola swerved to avoid the oncoming stagecoach, but managed to cover it with dust. "Bitch," yelled the guitar player, still perched on top of the stage. But the Black Widow, who was driving the stage, reined in her horses and whispered to no one in particular, "No bitch, that one. She is a witch—an evil one, here to destroy."

Nola slid her car to a halt, facing the wrong way in the turnaround circle, and the voice of Lou Rawls sang through her car speakers—"Let Me Be Good to You."

Calero froze, drawing himself up. His heart pounded, and once more his mind filled with the opening music of the *corrida*. He felt the sand beneath his feet, felt his mouth go dry.

Domingo and Parker witnessed the gathering storm. "The evil one has returned," Domingo muttered through clenched teeth.

Calero felt as if he were floating as he moved through the crowd toward the yellow Cadillac and the temptress at its controls. Three feet away from her, he stopped, anchored his feet, and spread his legs cowboy-style. His hands were poised at his sides, as if ready to draw on the enemy. Then he spoke. "Ma'am, this is horse country and folks don't take kindly to your speedin' machine...or your type."

Anger flashing in her eyes, nose tilting toward the darkening sky, Nola glared at Calero. Their stare-down ended when Nola finally spoke. "Well, you got what you wanted, didn't you?"

Calero's right hand moved across his body to where his pistol usually hung. Drawing his hand back, simulating it holding a revolver, he pointed it at her and pretended to fire. "Bang!" he said, and dropped his thumb as though it were the hammer. Bringing his imaginary gun to his lips, he blew imaginary smoke in her face. "You've got that right, lady. Now back this piece of yellow shit out of my life."

Nola's head dropped and her eyes blurred with tears, but Calero had already turned away. As he did, the stagecoach pulled even with him and the Black Widow leaned down to ask, "Need me to cast a spell on that dust-spewing garbage?"

"No...I don't need a spell." Even as he spoke, Calero felt a deepening sense of peace.

"Then send her away for good...never go near her." The Black Widow was vehement.

"She's already gone. I blew her away."

"She has not finished with you. See!"

Calero turned in time to see Nola get out of her car and come charging at him. Stopping abruptly, she stamped her foot. "You lowlife," she screamed. "Come to me! Now!"

Calero froze. He felt weak. He couldn't turn to face her.

"You don't walk away from me. Don't you ever walk away from Nola Rodriguez." She was wearing what he had called her "suit-of-lights," and she challenged him. "Come here...*toro*...where you belong."

Calero, filled with hatred, turned to face her then. In his mind, he could see the bull charge and tear through the *matadora*, tossing her high in the air. And then the goring, the goring and the goring. I want to charge her so bad. I want to kill her now! Rage welled in his chest and his face flushed with blood.

Then he heard it—Domingo's penetrating voice. *"Don* Calero. Mustachio! You requested your horse, *senor.* Here he is." Domingo led the horse closer, turning him so that all Calero had to do was mount and ride away for his life.

Calmed by Domingo's understanding act, Calero was once more in control—able to face Nola. He breathed deeply. "Good show, good theatrics, nice outfit," he told her, "but you'll never get what you want, Nola, because you're in the wrong arena. I'm not your problem. It's in your own head. Get it fixed. Stop being a killer of bulls, a killer of men. It won't bring your father back; won't bring you the happiness you've longed for."

Nola broke down at his words. "Why, Calero? Why can't we be together again?" Nola was begging as the tears spilled down her cheeks.

"Because we would destroy each other. Now go...and don't come back. I'm leaving the arena forever. I've just retired." Moments passed. He watched as Nola, staring at him, finally accepted him at his word. Returning to her car, she stomped on the gas pedal and roared away out of his life.

"Domingo, my good friend, thank you...*mil gracias.* Would you please ask the *mariachis* to play *'Nino Perdido'?*"

"Ah, yes. *'Nino Perdido'*—'The Lost Child.' Sometimes we feel like that when we lose a woman, eh?"

"*Tal vez*...but this time I'd like to hear it for my poor lost Spooky...and for all the lost children of the world."

"*Inmediatamente, senor.*" Domingo bowed and, taking his hat off, made a low cape pass as Calero trotted Buck slowly past him. "Today I think we win, *Don* Calero."

"There will be no winning or losing from now on, Domingo. I choose to never enter the arena again. I have retired." Calero smiled down at his old friend. "Take care of our guests for me, Domingo. I feel the need for a good ride!" Then he whirled his horse around and galloped past the stables, over the bridge, and up Sinnobar Hill.

23

Plaza de Toros

It was hot, it was Sunday, and Dr. Sidney Parker knew it would be the last time he and Calero would enter the arena together. Driving onto the Santa Clara campus, he parked by Noble Hall and trudged up the stairs to the third floor. He stopped in front of the door marked Counseling Center. How many times had Calero come through these doors over the years? Countless.

Parker took a deep breath and went into the waiting room. Good! None of his staff had come in on the weekend. He and Calero would be alone.

Leaving the front door ajar, he went into his office. It was only 3:30 P.M.—he still had half an hour. He put water for coffee on, then took the old record from its well-worn jacket and placed it on the record-changer. Taking his seat in the black leather swivel chair, he stared at the record jacket with its compelling picture of a matador caping a furious bull.

Waiting for the hands of the clock to reach precisely 4 P.M., Parker drifted into reminiscences about his remarkable patient and the significance of his past few sessions with Calero.

Sometimes I feel that I am Calero, he thought. I shift back and forth between the man Mustachio as lost little boy, as helpless man, rejected man, and all the other themes of pulling and pushing and struggle—and of course, of the bliss. Each one of us is a composite of all of these things, he thought. I believe that, possibly, all men are Calero at various times in their lives.

Parker glanced at the clock. There was still time and he went on with his thoughts. No one would have dreamed Calero's greatest secret was his taking the back roads to my office to share the struggles of his life and to find out who he was.

He traded the barn, the hay bales, the front porch, and the high hills—where he rode so often to explore his feelings and his pain—for a very new arena. He traded all of those one day, in desperation, for this couch in my office. He was determined to be free—and all that he could be. He was willing to pay any price.

It was only a few months ago that I told Calero his story should be known. It could help other men to better understand their own problems.

"I don't care if anybody understands me, Doc," he had said, "I am who I am, and I understand."

And I had answered him. "Yes, I see that. But I'm talking about other men like you. Other men struggling to be all they can be. Men who should have been born and bred in another age—who always feel like they are fish out of water, pilots out of their planes, or matadors out of the bullring. Do you know what I mean, Mustachio?" And I remember adding, "Excuse me for calling you that."

"You've been doing that a lot lately, Doc," he had replied.

And I smiled then and said, "I notice that when I do, you no longer reach to your left side as if to pull a gun or draw a sword. Does that mean you've really let me in?"

"Look, *pendejo*. If you're not in, nobody's in." Calero had returned my smile, and our conversation had continued.

"Mil gracias, senor Don Mustachio."

"Get off it, Doc."

"Anyway, the world is filled with men who seem to come from a time warp, from the past. Your story could help them. They're men bleeding from within but with no idea how the sword pierced them."

I recall Calero stiffening on the couch, turning to me and asking, "There really are men like that?"

"Yep. All good men enter the arena and pursue the impossible dream—or woman—at some stage of their lives. Some never live to tell the tale and some, like you, go to the arena over and over again only to take the sword in the heart still one more time."

I remember Calero nodded then and said, "Well, then, you have my permission to tell my story. Go ahead, use my name—make a TV series for all I care. Get rich."

"You'd give me, your shrink, that right?"

"What do I care? I have it all now. I feel together, a whole person. I feel like I can live in the past, live in the present, and yes, I can live for the future."

"Mustachio, you are like so many of my patients," I told him. "You've passed me by—you've moved ahead."

So Calero was getting better, beginning to laugh at his neurosis, and he no longer cared who knew his story. Now here it was Sunday, he was due any moment, and I would once more play the old record of *corrida* music.

It was after the crisis on the mountain, where Calero came so close to death, that he changed. Nola's spell over him was broken. He had announced, "I've decided not to die until I'm very old. But, when I do go, family tradition dictates I do it in the arena like *Grande Padre Mustachio.* My final Sunday will be my own Sunday. I will be alone—no music, no crowd. Do you know why this is important to me?

"I want to go like my grandfather—all alone, fighting the last bull. The horns ripped through his body and he dropped the cape and fell to his knees. The bull turned and charged one last time, ripped into his back and then threw him high into eternity. There were no *oles*. There was nothing but the stunned silence of the Spanish evening. My grandfather was dead when he hit the wet grass. I loved my grandfather." Tears had slipped down Calero's cheeks then.

"He lived a long life, didn't he?" I had asked.

"Yes, a long full life."

"And Domingo reminds you of him?"

"Yes, he does. And so do you, Doc, so do you."

"How old was your grandfather when he died?" I couldn't remember what Calero had told me earlier.

"The night he walked out alone into the pasture of bulls, that magnificent old man was seventy-five years old."

"Didn't he take his famous cape back to Spain with him, the one he always used in his great victories?"

"Yes, he took it. He retired as a famous bullfighter—a great bullfighter. He had won it all—fame, fortune, and best of all, my grandmother. He retired from the bullring and never went back, until the final curtain of his life began to fall. That night, the night of the last *corrida*, he caped his bull, then gave himself up to it. That's the way I want to leave this world."

The sound of my office clock striking four roused me from my thoughts and I spoke aloud, "It's four o'clock, Calero. Where are you?"

"Talking to yourself, Doc?" He was there, entering my office right on time. He took a chair instead of his usual place on the couch. "That's bad. You forgot to put the music on, too. You're slipping, Doc."

I jumped up, the record jacket falling to the floor, the thoughts I'd had receding away. Momentarily, I was embarrassed. "Calero! I didn't hear you come in."

"No more of my grand entrances, Doc. I've retired from the ring for the duration." Calero opened the box he held on his lap, pulled out a familiar bronze statue and placed it on the coffee table.

"Ah, the old lady's gift," I commented, leaning closer to study it more carefully. "Exquisite! The matador is as delicate as a woman."

"It is a woman, Doc. It's a *matadora*. It makes the final point that the bullfight isn't what it appears on the surface. The matador is a thinly disguised woman, and the bull is the man. The bull in the ring is like a proud man who falls in love—or lust—with the wrong woman. The more he wants from the object of his desire, the less he gets, and then rage replaces the fear of losing her. Once that happens, both bulls and foolish men earn their destruction.

"Nola was the wrong woman for me. We were very much alike, and when we came together, we became an explosive mixture. You can see it all there in the statue. See the bull wound round her feet and almost lost in the cape—her skirt? That's Nola and I. If I had known then what I've learned since, I would have seen things so obvious to me now."

Calero shook his head and frowned. "When Nola would get angry with me, she'd stamp her foot like the matador does to attract the bull. Once, after making love, she even called me her 'little beast.' She laughed at my mustache, asked me to shave it off. Said it scratched when we kissed. So, I shaved it off. Then her love turned to contempt for me as a man. Whenever I think that maybe I could still handle her, I just take this statue and hold it up to my face, like this." Calero lifted the statue and stared at it.

"So, I have taken the advice of that wise old man, Domingo: 'Get a good woman like your grandmother—one who gives you chocolate milk, not shit.' That good woman is my beloved Karin."

Calero smiled at me and went on, "And then, I apply the advice of that old philosopher, Doc Parker: 'Listen to the messages from your unconscious. Make friends with it. Then you won't need someone else to make you feel whole.'

"You know, Doc, gifts have been hard for me to accept— ever since my father died. He gave me things, but I wanted his love and praise. I give gifts freely, but I can't accept them easily. But I must if I'm to free myself from the past. The old lady helped me a lot with that. I couldn't refuse a gift she gave me from the grave."

"A fine gift from a fine woman." I said it softly, with respect.

"But the statue was only part of the gift, Doc. *Grande Padre Mustachio* would have been proud of me—the moves I made to win the final fight and live to retire. It was great theater, Doc, and the audience never knew—that's how well I did it. Through all the struggles, all the problems, I never played my trump card until the very end. I finally executed a perfect Pacheco Pass, and at precisely the right time. I knew the horns couldn't touch me.

"You see, Doc, I fought the ultimate bullfight. I went into that arena, but I didn't go like my father...I went like my grandfather. I had the magic cape. I knew I would win! I knew I had already won. Can you imagine what a thrill it was to fight the most dangerous bull of my life? To bring him as close to my heart and guts as I possibly could, yet knowing I was invincible—that the results of the *corrida* were preordained! That was my bullfight, Doc. I had the magic cape, and I could make the Pacheco Pass and live."

I sat fascinated—spellbound by Calero as always, but confused by his words.

"Remember when I told you the old lady had given me the statue and some other presents, Doc? Did I ever tell you that part of the present was land? Priceless land?"

I know my eyebrows went up. "No Calero, you didn't tell me that."

"Well, that land is the hill, Doc! It's the whole fucking hill!"

I moved forward in my chair. "The hill? Sinnobar Hill?"

"Yeah. So, if the county wanted to flood the low land, I was just going to move Judge Cash's house up to the top of that hill. I'd be able to sit out on that porch, just like the judge used to do, and look at an even bigger lake. But, as it turned out, the Triangle Sand and Gravel Company didn't want the valley—didn't care about the town and the water. They wanted the hill with its mineral deposits—gold deposits. But, I owned it all along.

"So, you see, I didn't really have to risk it with the final bull. I could kneel down in front of him like my grandfather did. I could feel the hot breath from the bull's nostrils on the back of my neck—just as my grandfather once did—and I knew he could never hook me, never throw me, he could never kill me. So, that's how I became the last great Mustachio."

"Son of a bitch! All the time, you owned the whole god-damned hill?" I slapped the arm of my chair.

"You got it, Doc."

"You mean to tell me that even when Nola was ready to rip your damned heart out, and I was struggling here to keep you from blowing your brains away, you already owned the hill?"

"Right, *gringo*." Calero grinned.

"Well, you son of a bitch! Why didn't you tell me?"

"I didn't tell you, Doc, because you needed to cape a few bulls of your own, didn't you? You needed to have a real tough case. Tell me this. The first time I came in here, did you really hear the music? Did you know it would be a great four o'clock in the afternoon? When you first came to the

ranch and started riding horses, you were as burned out and
bored as anybody I'd ever seen."

I found myself smiling at Calero's insight.

"This way, Doc, we both caped our bulls, and fought in
the big arena. I needed you, you needed me. I'll admit I made
a few unorthodox passes. I may even have scared the hell out
of myself, and you. Maybe I even felt like running away
from this life. But, you know, the people loved it."

"What people, Mustachio?"

"The people in my mind," Calero explained. "Because,
for me, the struggle outside was nothing like the struggle in
the arena of my mind. I could have won everything in the
outside world, but I almost lost it in the inside arena. If I had
lost, all the people in my mind would have gone down with
me. The horns of the bull would have swept the stands clean.
There would have been nothing left but torn seat cushions,
spilled beer, dead *picadors* and bleeding horses. But I won,
Doc, and so, as they say—*Ole!*"

I was still curious. "Any other reason why you carried
this on when you could have ended it at any moment? You
owned the hill…"

"Because every man loves a good fight. And people love
the theatre, a rodeo, a magic show—young or old, smart or
dumb. You, too, Doc. So I caped the bulls in my mind—for
the fun and thrills, for the knowledge, for the entertainment."

"*Ole*, you Spanish bastard. But you can't fool me. You
never caped in a bull that close to you before, and wearing
your heart on your naked arm as well! Come on, Calero."

"God, it was close, wasn't it? I was fighting blind in the
beginning, and I was good, but then I became fearful,
angry…fatalistic. I realized that perhaps I wasn't a great
fighter…and that just about killed me. It hurt so bad not to be
like *Grande Padre Mustachio.*

"But, I kept fighting, looking for the key, and you and Domingo helped me. You gave me gifts I had to accept if I wanted to live. I'm grateful, Doc, to both of you. I realize now that a great fighter must know he can win. He understands his own skills and those of his opponent thoroughly. He can have no illusions—they can kill. Grandfather took no unnecessary risks in the bullring, but he made it appear risky and dangerous. He always knew he had the skills necessary for handling the bulls.

"Play the last part of that record, Doc. It's the music that's played when a fighter leaves the arena in triumph." Calero got up from his chair and put the statue of the *matadora* back in its box.

I realized I wanted to prolong the session. "What about the recurrent dream that has tortured you for so long?"

"Oh, that dream. Well, it finally completed itself with me marching out of the ring behind my grandfather. My father was there, too, beside me, and we were equals. The victory music was playing and I knew a golden-haired woman was waiting for me—my Karin."

I rose then and hugged Calero affectionately. Stepping back, I said, "Two ears for you, Calero."

He grinned as he said, "And a tail and a hoof for you, Doc."

"Adios, Mustachio. I know I'm going to miss you."

"So long, *gringo.*" He gave me a last salute, then he was gone.

24

The Last Lonely Ride

Buck, his horse, stood ready just as he had requested. Domingo and two *braceros* were tending the horses. The Sunday morning air smelled fresh, and, after taking a deep breath, Calero turned away from the bedroom window. He was alone again, but free. Sweet Karin was in the air, bound for Spain. "Godspeed, beautiful one," he whispered. Then he dressed slowly.

In the kitchen, he blasted a cup of leftover coffee in the microwave before going out to Buck. The horse nuzzled him in recognition, spilling Calero's coffee. Once mounted, Calero rode past the hay barn and waved to Domingo. "Love that man," he said to the horse. "Without him, Buck, I'd be nowhere and someone else would be your *patron*."

The place was deserted. No boarders' cars were parked by the barn. Good. It was too early for them—or was it? Out by the back stalls, someone was moving about. Calero rode toward the muffled noise. "I'll be damned," he muttered, "if it isn't Doc Parker the Shrink." Then more loudly, "What'd you do, Doc, sleep here all night with that mare of yours?"

"Morn'n,' Calero," Parker said, as he continued to groom his horse. "Left my car at the gate and walked in. Sort of for old times' sake."

Calero disappeared up the trail, and Sidney Parker flashed back once again to that earlier day, ten years ago, when he had first come to the ranch. There was the old water tank high on the hill, just as it had been for maybe a hundred years, dwarfed now by the modern tank with the words *BIENVENIDO*, WELCOME TO RANCHO CALERO.

The old and the new were now a blend. Back then, there had been only a tumble-down barn or two—and a man named Calero and his dream. Now there were renovated barns and new stalls, and horse-trailers waiting so boarders could take their horses off to some obscure California trail. Ever-present and loyal *braceros* squatted down, resting and waiting for orders from their *patron*. The barns, the earthy smells, the *braceros* speaking in Spanish all took Parker back to an earlier California. He wondered if Calero would have been happier then, and thought that probably he would.

He walked through the stalls, patting a horse's outstretched muzzle here and there. Lost in the past, he was startled out of his reverie when he came upon a Mexican apparently talking to the side of the barn. After a moment, he laughed at himself. He realized the man was talking on a telephone that had been mounted unobtrusively against the barn's side.

Parker realized that Calero had seen to it that everything of the past was carefully preserved so that the present would intrude as little as possible. The Calero touch was obvious everywhere on the ranch. He had saved what was best from the past.

Noticing a dust cloud being kicked up along the lane, Parker wondered at its cause. Wild *vaqueros* charging down the lane? It was a car intruding on the old California West, and Parker realized that no matter how early in the day he might come to the ranch, he couldn't escape back into the old times for long. He looked up at Calero, high on the hill now—a lonely rider from another time, looking huge even from a distance.

High on his hill, Calero was looking down on the ranch and talking to his horse. "It's beautiful up here, Buck. It's all ours now…but so what? No Spooky nipping at our heels…no woman here to share it all with me. I'm forty-nine years old and single to boot. I've had to accept a lot this year…damn near killed me. Lost my fantasies, lost that temptress, Nola. And maybe I've lost the perfect mate in Karin. I lost the old lady, too. I've gained everything material…and lost everything of the heart.

"You know, Buck, what I miss most of all? What makes me feel the most lonesome? It's the loss of the struggle." Calero paused and thought for a moment. "I think it's the meeting of danger head on, caping it close…winning by just enough margin to be able to fight again. You know something, Buck…sometimes insight and self-understanding suck. They suck the mystery, the drama, the danger, the theater out of life."

He quieted the restless horse. "Stand still, dammit, and listen to me, Buck! I guess I understand my father better now, too. He felt he could do anything as long as he had that mysterious woman's approval and favors. He didn't know what hit him. His vision was clouded by her femininity and seductive ways. He must have floated through his days before that great fight in Tijuana. I think he must have felt complete in every way…as long as he had her. Then he went into the arena that fateful day, only to die whispering her name…without ever having any insight, Buck.

"I see now why he did that, why many men do that—especially young men, men without experience. But for it to happen to a man like me? A forty-nine-year-old! Give me a break. Time to grow up and grow old. End the game playing. Be like *Grande Padre Mustachio,* not my father. Live a good life. Don't end up an old fool."

Calero's mutterings to his horse were suddenly interrupted. "What the hell is that, Buck? Another runaway horse? Can't be a runaway, it's running up the trail. An out-of-control horse would head for the barn. But that horse is smoking, although the rider certainly knows how to ride. Where do these damn *gringos* come from?"

"Mustachio! Mustachio!"

"What the…?" He reached for his rifle. "Mustachio?" He slumped back in the saddle grumbling. "God, I hate that name! Who the hell is on my case now?"

Out of his sight, around a bend in the trail, a voice yelled again, "Mustachio! Mustachio!" He could tell, then, that it was a woman's voice, and out of the dust came a charging horse, its rider leaning into the wind, whipping her mount with her hat.

Buck stamped his feet, quivering with excitement, and Calero's heart leapt as Karin and her horse closed the last few yards between them at breakneck speed.

Skidding her horse to a sudden stop, Karin promptly made an announcement, "I love you, and I refuse to go to Spain without you."

"What?!" Calero was disbelieving.

"Spain! We go together or I don't go at all."

"No, not that…the other part."

"Oh, that. I said I loved you…and, Mustachio, we should always be together no matter what…I love you very much."

Calero's face crumpled into a happy grin. "Sounds like a lifelong commitment."

"It is, Mustachio, it is."

"Hey, you know I hate that name."

"Well, I love it, and I love you, and you'll just have to get used to it."

"Speaking of commitment, Karin, where would you like to get married…Spain or here…and when?" Calero was smiling broadly now.

"Here, and as soon as possible. Right on this spot. Just a few people." Karin moved her horse closer to him and reached over to touch his cheek, the love on her face plain for him to see.

"Then we'll go to Spain to honeymoon…for as long as you need to do your thing. That excites me, Karin, helping you do what you want to do. I'll have a new arena this time…but with tame bulls and nothing to prove. I like that idea—it feels good."

"Me, too, Mustachio-*mio*. By the way, how about some frosting on your cake?"

"Of course. What's a wedding cake without frosting?"

"No, I mean right now." Karin gave out a piercing whistle that made Calero wince.

"Jesus, that hurts! Can you teach me how to do that?"

Karin ignored him as she turned to face downhill. "Domingo! Domingo!" she shouted through her cupped hands, and Calero saw Domingo wave back at Karin from the barn below.

"All right, Karin, what's that all about?"

"The frosting!" And she pointed down the trail.

Calero saw a dog making its way up the hill, heard a familiar bark, and knew immediately it was his beloved Spooky. "Spooky! They found him. He's come back!" Bursting with delight, he leaned over to give Karin a kiss. They dismounted and held each other hungrily as Spooky, barking joyously, tore up to them.

Spanish/English Glossary

adios .... good-bye
agua .... water
ahora .... now
alto .... stop
amiga .... female friend
amigo .... male friend
andale .... hurry
aqui .... here
a sus ordenes ..... at your service
atras .... behind

_____

bandoleer .... large leather belt worn over one shoulder, across chest, containing receptacles for bullets
bienvenido .... welcome
bracero .... laborer
buena vista .... nice view
buenas noches ... good night
buenas tardes ..... good afternoon, good evening
buenos dias .... good morning

_____

casita .... little house

cerveza .... beer
cojones .... testicles
como se llama .... what is your name
corrida de toros .... bullfight
compadre .... friend
comprende .... understand
con su permiso .... with your permission

_____

Dios .... God
Dios mio .... my God
Dios solo comprende ..... only God knows
Don .... title of respect—large land owner
Dos Equis .... brand name of beer

_____

el toro mucho malo .... very bad bull
es verdad .... it is true

_____

feliz .... happy

_____

fiesta brava .... great party
fuera .... get out

_____

gordo .... fat
gracias .... thank you
grande .... large
gringo .... foreign, Yankee, fair-haired
guerra puerto .... war room

_____

hombre .... man
huevos .... eggs
huevos rancheros .... Mexican-style eggs

———————

Ingles .... English
inmediatemente .... immediately

———————

limon .... lemon, lime
listo ahora .... ready now
Los Gatos .... the cats

———————

mano a mano .... hand to hand
mariachi .... authentic music of Mexico—
                                             origin 1860, during Emperor
                                             Maximilian's reign
matador .... bullfighter
matadora .... female bullfighter
me nina necessita leche .... my baby girl needs milk
me casa es su casa .... my house is your house
mesero .... waiter
mi amigo, amiga .... my friend
mil gracias .... a million thanks
mio .... my, mine
mucho gusto en conocerlo .... glad to meet you
muchos problemas .... many problems
muy pronto .... very quickly
muerto hombre .... dead man
muleta .... red cape
mustachio .... mustache
muy listo ahora .... very ready now

———————

nada .... no, nothing, none

---

oficionado .... official
ole .... bravo, well done

---

passe .... pass
patron .... boss
pendejo .... cowardly, dumb, stupid, jerk
pequeno .... little
permitame .... allow me
picador .... a horseman who participates in
the early part of a bullfight by
irritating and enraging the bull
with slight thrusts of a lance
plaza de toros .... bullring
por favor .... please

---

senor .... mister
Senor Feliz .... Mr. Happy (slang for penis)
senora .... missus
senorita .... miss

---

tal vez .... possibly
tiene una cerveza para me ... have a beer for me
torero .... bullfighter
toro .... bull
toro mierda .... bullshit

---

vaquero .... cowboy